Elizabeth R. Charles

Ewan Christian

Architect

Elizabeth R. Charles

Ewan Christian
Architect

ISBN/EAN: 9783742820228

Printed in Europe, USA, Canada, Australia, Japan

Cover: Foto ©Andreas Hilbeck / pixelio.de

More available books at **www.hansebooks.com**

Yours very truly
Ewan Christian

Ewan Christian,

ARCHITECT.

PRINTED FOR PRIVATE CIRCULATION.

Cambridge:

PRINTED AT THE UNIVERSITY PRESS.

1896

Our friend has gone to his well-earned rest—gathered to the great harvest like a sheaf of corn fully ripe—surrounded by all those things which should accompany old age, as "love, honour, obedience, troops of friends," leaving us to chronicle and to cherish the fresh, green memory of his genial, kindly presence; bequeathing to us the bright example of the kind and courteous Christian gentleman, the enthusiastic lover of his art, the honourable and honoured architect, and what more can I say, or what more would he have wished to be said of him than, "Let me die the death of the righteous, and let my last end be like his."

(From Mr Christian's Presidential Address at the R.I.B.A., 2 Nov. 1885—referring to the late Prof. Donaldson.)

CONTENTS.

INTRODUCTION.

THOSE of us who feel that a bit of the sunshine of life passed away with the tidings that we should never again have the cordial greetings and the cheering presence of Mr Christian in our homes, cannot but rejoice that, before the echoes of his kind voice have grown fainter, some record of that high and gracious character should be preserved for us, and spread further among those who only knew him through his work.

The memory of lives lived fully, to the very last—in keenness of intellectual power, in faithful carrying out of duty, in freshness of heart for all dear ties of relationship and friendship,—is indeed among our most precious "Intimations of Immortality."

Enthusiasm for all that is highest, carried out in faithful work through a noble career from youth to age, is an inspiration for the young, and an illumination through the shadows of age for those who are growing old.

And, besides this general human reason for welcoming a sketch of Mr Christian's life, there is the special reason for it, on account of the great opportunities he had, as a leading member of the profession of the great Builders, of linking the Present with the Past, not by a servile copying of the work of olden times, but by a free fulfilling of the spirit, and a faithful treading in the footsteps of the workers. Delight in designing,—thoroughness in working,—wideness of grasp with minute care for detail,—reverence for the beauty of the past, with freedom in adapting the methods of the past to the circumstances of the present,—all this can be best estimated by those who can understand the difficulties he met and conquered, whether in restoration of ancient work, or in original designs of his own; in the restoration of Cathedrals, or in the new National Portrait Gallery (now all but completed), the plans of which were among the last things on which his dying eyes rested.

Victor Hugo[1] has said, *le livre tuera l'édifice.* But "the Book" need not "kill the Building," as long as there are Builders left who can make Books of their Buildings,—sacred or secular,—who can express their own best thoughts, and those of their age, through what they build, giving us "sermons in stones," because they themselves have found "God in everything."

ELISABETH RUNDLE CHARLES.

[1] In his *Notre Dame de Paris.*

CHAPTER I.

LIFE.

Who is the honest man?
He that doth still and strongly good pursue,
To God, his neighbour, and himself most true:
Whom neither force nor fawning can
Unpin, or wrench from giving all their due.

GEORGE HERBERT.

THE Portrait which forms the frontispiece of this little book is a copy of a life-sized crayon[1] sketch drawn in the year 1876 by Mr George Richmond, R.A., at his own desire, in gratitude for certain friendly services. In writing to present the picture to Mrs Christian, the artist thus expresses himself, "I am not always pleased with my own work: but in this sketch I felt that I had not wholly missed the grace and sweetness of my model." To many who knew and loved Mr Christian well, it will seem, perhaps, that 'grace and sweetness' are hardly the fittest words with which to characterize him: that he impressed them rather with a sense of

---

[1] Another portrait, painted by Mr W. W. Ouless, R.A. in 1886, is in the possession of the Royal Institute of British Architects.

force and decision, of a vehemence ever ready to
break out from restraint, of a spirit earnest and lofty,
but approaching somewhat to severity, and even stern-
ness. Yet grace and sweetness there were, in the
countenance as in the character,—the grace of a pure
soul, the sweetness of refinement and warmth of
heart,—for those who had, like the artist, an eye to
discern them, and a congenial spirit to draw them
out from their habitual reserve.

The signature which stands below the portrait
symbolizes well the union of old and new ; the name
and worth of an ancient family descent, with the
strong individuality of its living representative. The
name of " Christian " belongs to the Isle of Man, and
in its earlier form, *McChristen*, preserves the memory
of the time when the Scandinavian invaders of the
9th and 10th centuries, mingling with the Celtic
population of the island, adopted their Celtic pre-
fixes. The name " Ewan," or as it is sometimes spelt,
"Huan," is probably a Celtic form of " John," and has
been borne by some member of the family in almost
every generation. In 1408 one John McChristen was
Deemster or Judge in the Isle of Man, and in 1422
was still a member of the Tynwald Court. In 1511
his third successor, John McChristen, also Deemster,
purchased the estate of Milntown in the parish of
Lezayre. Five generations later, Ewan, who became
Deemster in 1605 at the age of 26, and held the office
for 51 years, changed the family name to its present

form, *Christian.* He was Deputy Governor of the Island and Constable of Peel Castle, and in his time the Earl of Derby, "King in Man," writing of the Christian family, says, "they have made themselves chief here." The William Christian known by Manxmen as "Illiam Dhoan,"— "Brown William,"—who is introduced by Sir Walter Scott into *Peveril of the Peak*[1], was his son. The great-grandson of the above-named Constable, also Ewan, added the estate of Ewanrigg in Cumberland to that of Milntown, and is noted in the Bishop's visitation as a generous friend to the Church, restoring to the poor Vicar of Deerham the corn-tithes which belonged to himself as Impropriator. This Ewan Christian was succeeded in 1719 by his son John[2], whose descendants represent the elder branch of the family. A younger son, Thomas, became Vicar of Crossthwaite in the Lake Country, in 1728, a man of strong and independent character, who established his son Joseph in business in London. In the next generation a second Joseph Christian married his cousin Katharine, daughter of

[1] Readers of this novel will remember that William Christian is represented (not unfairly) as a man who took a leading and tragic part in the troubled events of the day, and whose memory was very differently regarded by the opposing factions. The 'Edward Christian' of the tale, however, is avowedly no portrait at all, but 'a mere creature of the imagination.'

[2] Of this John Christian one grandson became Lord Ellenborough: another was Fletcher Christian, who headed the mutineers of the 'Bounty,' and left descendants in Pitcairn, subsequently transferred to Norfolk Island.

Mr John Scales of Thwaitehead in Lancashire, and died in 1821, leaving nine children; of these the seventh was Ewan, to whose memory the following pages are lovingly dedicated.

Mr Ewan Christian was born in London on Sept. 20, 1814. Of his infancy and early years we have occasional glimpses in his mother's letters. These letters, written in a full and graceful epistolary style, more common formerly than now, show Mrs Christian to have been a woman of singular beauty of character, refined, unaffected, warm-hearted towards all except, perhaps, "artificial people." Her practical wisdom in the affairs of daily life was penetrated through and through by the earnestness of Christian faith, and by a sympathetic love of Nature in all its various aspects, especially of her native Lake Country. To her "dearest Christian" she was a true and loyal wife, to all her children a wise and tender mother. Though she died when he was but eight years old, Mr Christian cherished his mother's memory with chivalrous affection, and it is not difficult to see how much he owed to her. Of him at the age of three months she says, "my dear babe is grown so fine a fellow"; and again, writing from her step-sister's beautiful home at Casterton, she describes his enjoyment of the country: "Dear Ewan" (now aged four) "is grown quite a rosy, hardy man: he helps Edward in the stable-yard, dines by his own choice at a side-table in the kitchen, and helps to milk the cows under the shade of those beautiful trees we see from the drawing-room window, and rides in the donkey-cart, with many more delights..." "As I write, I see going past in the shrubbery Ewan and Agnes wheeled by John in the wheelbarrow, which the gardener has left." About the same time; "Ewan will find it very soon too cool for nankeens," and is to have "a frock and trowsers the size of his plaid, of pepper and salt trimmed with black,"—in case the Queen (Charlotte) should die.

Mr Joseph Christian died in June, 1821, and his wife, whose health was failing, survived him but little more than a year. The grandparents, however, were still living at Mortlake. Their old-fashioned garden with its abundant fruit trees was one of the well-remembered delights of little Ewan's childhood, and they seem to have interested themselves much in his education. "Grandpapa," writes Miss Emma Christian (afterwards Mrs Wontner) in April, 1822, "thinks Ewan's abilities wonderful: whatever he applies himself to he will accomplish." There was some thought of sending him to St Paul's School, and of training him ultimately to take Holy Orders. But "Grand-papa and Grandmamma desire to get him into Christ's Hospital," as it was thought that the air of Hertford would be beneficial to a delicate child.

Accordingly at the age of eight (June, 1823) Ewan began his career in the junior branch of Christ's Hospital, established at Hertford. He used to speak in later days of the simple old-fashioned style of

living, and how the boys "slept the clock round."
His younger brother Joseph was also admitted to
Christ's Hospital in 1824, and becoming in course
of time a Grecian, proceeded to Pembroke Hall, Cambridge.   Of this early period of Ewan's boyhood little
can be discovered.   One of his younger contemporaries, the Rev. F. G. Nash[1], has given us this slight
sketch of his character at school.   "I was only nine
years old when he was fifteen.   The impression that
seems to have remained in my mind is that he had more
than usual influence among the other senior boys,
and that the juniors felt that they had in him a friend
and protector.   I cannot recall anything that he did
or said to account for this impression, and suppose
it must have arisen from his appearance and kindliness of manner."   One of the reminiscences of his
school days was that he took great interest in the
building of the Great Hall.   The area of the building operations was forbidden ground, but Ewan had a
little corner from which he could watch what was
going on unobserved, and the workmen would smuggle
him out to save him from punishment.   Thus early
were the instincts of the future architect discovered.

With all the gratitude which he felt to his old
school, Mr Christian never ceased to regret that in
his boyhood he had so few opportunities of being
acquainted with country life.   To the advantages
of such training he alludes long afterwards when

---

[1] Vicar of Clavering, Essex.

writing to his eldest daughter on the question of exchanging her rural home at Silsoe for the town life of Cambridge.

"THWAITEHEAD,
"15*th May*, 1887.

"Many a small country vicarage like yours has been the workshop and source of large instrumentalities of good. Bishop Fraser's best years were passed in smaller centres of usefulness, and yet his influence was as widely felt as that of any man of the present century. Richard Hooker minded the sheep on the glebe of a small vicarage, and in the quietude of his study produced immortal work, spite of the scoldings of the shrew to whom he was mated. . . . If there is anything I have regretted more than another in my course of life, it has been that I could not give my children the inestimable advantage of the education of a country life. I know what a loss it has been to myself to have been brought up in a town; how much I am ignorant of which might have been learnt by merely opening my eyes to the every-day sights and sounds of Nature's teachings, and certainly some of the most cultured people I have ever met, and some of the most learned men, have been found in what would be deemed by some country solitudes."

And again, in the latest letter which she received from him, he reverts to the same subject.

"THWAITEHEAD,
"25 *August*, 1894.

". . . . I enclose a cutting from the *Hampstead Express*, written, as I am told, by an 'Old Gardener.' I wish there were many like open-minded cultivators of the earth, with eyes and brains of the same sort. What I lost in my youth by the want of such teaching I have long and often keenly felt, but I rarely saw a flower or field till after I left school, though the delights of one month of August *just 70 years* since, I can still remember, for August 1824 I spent in a delightful farm-house with a very large garden, and most of my days in the harvest field. I have never known how it came about; but old Mrs Martin of Southery was a very kind motherly woman, and her husband a very fine specimen of the gentleman farmer. . . . I remember his face, even now, of bright intelligence. That was in the old days of coach travelling, when we dined at the 'Hoop' at Cambridge, and got to Southery, near Downham, to tea, and it was accounted very fast travelling at eight miles an hour! Now you will think it very odd that the sending of this newspaper extract should summon up such a store of recollections, but they come out naturally enough when I remember also the contrasting circumstances of burial in the bricks and stone and mortar, and no trees, flowers or insects, in the six years of Christ's Hospital, and never in contact with anyone who cared for country delights. . . . . The faculty of all others that it is important in my view to cultivate carefully is that of observation. 'Eyes and no Eyes' is a tale that ought to be written in letters of gold, for it just makes the difference between man and man, whether or not that faculty is brought out. I know it too well, for though I have acquired some power, it is not by any means so keen as I know it ought to be."

A few months after leaving school (1829, ætat. 15) he was articled to Mr Matthew Habershon, a London architect. It is interesting to note that his indentures are dated Sept. 20th—his birthday. At once he began to study hard for his profession. He became a student at the Royal Academy; and about the same time was attending the French lectures of M. Delisle at the London University. In 1832 he passed some time at Nottingham, engaged on work for Mr Habershon. A letter written by him to his sister, Mrs Lloyd, at Hawkshead, dated Oct. 24, 1834, shows us the young man full of energy and confidence at twenty years of age. He has been trying to get an appointment to superintend the building of a church at Clappersgate, and has sent in a design "on speculation." He is thinking of preparing also a design for a new church at Kendal, "in the hopes of stirring them up to build." He urges his sister to "keep her children at home, as her little chaps by being brought up in the North will (as all North countrymen do), be sure to get on" if they come to London. He then describes his first tour abroad, a visit he has lately made to Paris. In company with a friend, he started by the *Times* coach to Southampton. Arrived at Havre the next morning, he notices the picturesque houses chiefly built of wood, filled in with plaster, and apologizes for this "methodical stuff" instead of a description of the "sensations" usually felt, or "professed to be felt," on first landing in a foreign land, with the excuse "I have not much ideality in my composition, and I do not profess to feel what I really do not." The letter is however full of enthusiasm. The beauty of the Seine, illustrated by a slight sketch; the glory of the west front of Rouen Cathedral, and St Ouen's (though throughout the whole of his travels he has "seen nothing at all to compare to our own majestic Abbey," *i.e.* Westminster); the *diligence* to Paris (illustrated with diagrams); the approach to Paris by the Champs Elysées,—all come in for glowing description, notwithstanding his professed lack of "ideality." He is greatly impressed by the galleries of the Louvre, but thinks Notre Dame inferior to Saint Sulpice, and the Panthéon superior to St Paul's! From Paris the friends proceed to Orleans, which in its decay suggests the reflection, "how are the mighty fallen," and thence to Tours, where the grapes receive appreciative notice. From Tours, "by a conveyance called a Trycycle," they are taken along the high river bank to Saumur and Nantes, whence they turn their steps homeward. He calculates, characteristically, that he has travelled 1300 miles in three weeks, and brings his letter to a hasty finish, as he has a design in his head for the new Kendal Church[1], which he intends to commit to paper.

The next few years of his life were spent in professional work in various parts of the country, but it is not easy to arrange the events of this period in exact order of time. In 1835 he was searching out and sketching half-timbered houses in Lancashire, Cheshire and Shropshire for Mr Habershon's book on the subject. He spent some time with Mr Brown of Norwich, and was also employed at Colchester, where occurred an incident which he used to relate with great enjoyment,—how he detected some workmen laying down sand instead of concrete, watched them from a little window guiltily hurrying over their work, and then broke out upon them to their

---

[1] This design appears to have been exhibited in the Academy in 1835. See p. 57.

speechless discomfiture, with a thunderlike "You rascals!" In 1840 he helped Mr Railton to prepare his competitive designs for the new Houses of Parliament, and in 1841 we find him superintending the erection of Lee Church (for which he received an honorarium of 50 guineas), submitting designs and seeking posts in different places, and at home working often as much as 11 hours a day. At the same time he spent a night weekly at the Institute of British Architects, of which he had just become a member, and gave some hours regularly to lessons in French and Italian. In his diary the wind, thermometer, and weather are carefully registered day by day.

In October, 1841, he started for the tour to Rome and Naples, which formed an epoch in his life. His diary records his progress through France, and gives spirited descriptions of many portions of his route, such as the "magnificent country" between Paris and Chambéry, and the snowy crossing of Mt Cenis to Turin. With Turin he is disappointed at first, and finds the churches "unbearably offensive." Genoa (reached by "velociferi") he thinks "may be truly called superb, but the town is a labyrinth."

The following extract from his Notes describes his impressions in his own words :

Genoa. The situation of the city is truly beautiful, and the views in every direction from the ramparts, the heights above the town, or in any situation from which the sea is visible, are most splendid. It is completely shut in by the lofty hills behind, and the sea in front, and is strongly fortified. The hills, except close to the town where they are covered with olive trees and vines, are exceedingly bare and rocky, but from their beautiful and varied outlines offer great attractions to the admirer of nature unadorned ; and the prospects from the heights looking up the valleys, where here and there a little hamlet is placed, with its church tower built almost invariably upon an eminence, and appearing in the distance so peaceful and smiling, are truly enchanting. But to be appreciated and to produce their full effect, they must be seen when the bells are in motion, for nothing seems more in character with this description of scenery than the sound, far off, of "the church-going bell." To me, when alone and away from the bustle of men, it is perfect enjoyment to sit and drink in the beauties of nature, and listen to such sounds which are always, I think, calculated to produce a delightful and refreshing effect upon the mind.

At Genoa he spent a fortnight, detained by the difficulty of recovering his books, which the "set of unprincipled thieves, king and people," had taken from him at the frontier. Thence he started by steamer to Naples, but was driven by a gale to Spezzia ; and this led to further adventures, for having coasted to Leghorn, he and some fellow passengers made an excursion to Pisa. But on their return they found the sea so violent that their boat failed to reach the steamer. After a second and a third attempt the other passengers became alarmed and gave it up. Mr Christian went down a fourth time alone to persuade the boatmen to try again, but by this time the steamer had gone and he was "*détenu.*" However, two days later he succeeded in getting on. Eight days were spent at Naples busily, but without much occasion for comment in the diary. A few more days were occupied in a trip to the neighbourhood of Pæstum and Amalfi, the delight of which was keen with him for fifty years. On Thursday, Dec. 9th, he arrived at Rome.

At Rome he settled down for three months' work, seeing the city, making sketches, studying Italian, and amidst it all, devoting several mornings to designs for a church at Tonbridge, *i.e.* probably Hildenborough[1], where he built his first church in the following year. Memorials of his industry still remain in the form of a number of very careful pencil sketches, a closely written diary, and many pages of descriptive notes, partly written in Italian, studies for the most part of architectural buildings, but including also some impressions of scenery. Of these notes another extract may be given, as worthy of more than passing consideration.

Pæstum, Dec. 2nd....It is only by visiting and seeing them in their own proper atmosphere that one can appreciate the full beauty of the Grecian Temples. Setting aside all the interest attached to their antiquity, and their appropriate character as memorials of other customs and modes of worship, and considering them simply as masses of architecture, it is only in their clear atmosphere that all their beauty can be seen. No copy, however accurate, can give an idea of the extreme beauty of every portion whether in detail or mass. In every part the marks of close study are visible, and there

---

[1] Hildenborough is a village, then in the parish of Tonbridge.

can be no greater enjoyment than to endeavour by close attention to discover from them the meaning and intentions of their
authors.

While at Rome he also formed the friendship,
destined to ripen into lasting intimacy, of Mr (afterwards Professor) T. Hayter Lewis, and (Sir) Horace
Jones, by whose society his hitherto solitary life
must have been much enlivened. On one occasion
the three friends with four others formed a united
party, to make a four days' walking tour to Tivoli
and Frascati. On the third day they found themselves benighted at a little village called Calonna,
boasting only a very primitive albergo. " The rooms,"
writes Mr Lewis, "were unfurnished, they had no
beds, no mattrasses, no linen. But the night was
dark, the road difficult to find; there was a good
fire, and·very clearly some very good ham, so we
determined to stop. Accordingly we had some hay
laid on the brick floor, a thick cloth or something
of that kind laid over it, and there we all seven lay,
four on one side and three on the other, one's heels in
the other's face. It was cold outside and most dread-
fully hot in, for we had two thick coverlids over us.
However, we had had a good supper of broiled ham
and poached eggs, and got several hours of very
sound sleep." Many a good laugh was enjoyed over
this adventure by the friends in later times. And
more than 43 years afterwards, in June 1885, when
Mr Christian, as President of the Royal Institute of

British Architects, had occasion to receive on behalf
of the Institute the portrait of Sir Horace Jones, he
wove the reminiscence of the tour into his reply to
Mr Barry with singularly happy effect.

Horace Jones is one of my oldest friends. You did not
include my name amongst those who met him in Rome, but
Hayter Lewis and I, with Horace Jones, are the only surviving
members of that party of young fellows who walked the Cam-
pagna forty-three years ago, and studied with all the zeal that
we could the great works that we found in Rome and elsewhere.
It is a great pleasure to me to see that picture here. It is
not exactly the portrait of the young gentleman who sat
side by side with me, sketching a palace of Bramante, and
appointing Hayter Lewis as the arbitrator of our sketches, but
it is the same genial face, in the portrait of the substantial
city magnate that we see before us, that I remember of old,
and have known all through my professional life as one of my
best friends, and therefore it is a peculiar pleasure to me to be
able on this occasion to receive that portrait.

There are a great many young men present here, some to
whom I have presented medals, and one to whom I suggested
the possibility of occupying this chair in the future, and I am
able to tell them a remarkable thing,—that out of a party of
seven, three, the only three remaining members of that party
of students, have occupied this chair as Vice-President. If
it had not been for our friend Professor Lewis' health, which
would not allow him to take office as President—and he would
have been a most popular President amongst us—we should
probably all have occupied the presidential chair.

Therefore I think it is worth mentioning, and may be some
encouragement to the young men on the benches behind, to
think what is before them. If any kind angel had whispered
to me, "You will be occupying the great chair which the
Institute has to bestow," I should have dismissed him with
the contemptuous remark that it was utterly impossible, but

here I am, and if some of the young men that I see before me will follow out their profession as Professor Hayter Lewis and Horace Jones have done, and with all the energy and zeal of their characters, and never lose any opportunity of learning whatever they can, as Dr Schliemann[1] has done, they may also come to occupy this chair, and I hope they will.

The Roman visit came to an end. On March 3rd, 1842, Mr Christian said goodbye to the Eternal City, and to his friends there. On his return he visited Florence, Bologna, Venice and Milan, and having crossed the Simplon to Paris, arrived in London on May 7th. It was characteristic of him that while he was away he kept a minutely accurate account, both of his expenditure and of the number of miles travelled each day, of which the following is his summary:

No. of miles, 3377. Coach-fare and all conveyances £40, or 2·84*d.*, nearly, per mile.

Time, 30 weeks. Expenses of lodging &c. £65. 7*s.*, or 4·6*d.*, nearly, per mile, or £3. 10*s.* 3*d.* per week.

The end of the year 1842 saw Mr Christian installed at No. 6, Bloomsbury Square[2], as a residence and place of business on his own account. His habits were then, as they always continued to be, very simple. He rose early, and, after drinking a glass of water,

---

[1] Dr Schliemann was also present to receive the Gold Medal of the Institute.

[2] A very fine house at the corner of Hart Street (now No. 5) in which Isaac Disraeli once lived.

would "take a run round the Squares" before breakfast, usually with a book in his hand. This practice
of a morning walk he was wont to recommend to his
friends as a panacea for all ailments, and the instinct
was still strong in him in all seasons, winter and
summer, to the end of his life. To this period of his
life he may have referred when in the course of a
discussion at the Institute (in 1885) on the York
Water-gate[1], he said, "I think it a very beautiful
building...and I am old enough to remember it as
a real approach to the river. In my young days I
was very fond of boating, and frequently passed
under it on my way to the water." He worked till
late at night, and would often ask his first pupil,
Mr C. H. Purday, who entered his office in 1845, to
come in and write in the evening after office hours,
and frequently also to take away some dimensions to
'square up' before breakfast the next morning. His
frame was strong and elastic. He is described already
as carrying his head slightly bent forward like one
absorbed in thought. And owing to a temporary
weakness of the eyes, contracted, or aggravated, by
close application to minute drawings, such as those
with which he had lately been helping Mr Railton,
he had already begun to wear the broad-brimmed
style of hat long familiar to his friends. While resident

---

[1] A fragment of a Palace built by Inigo Jones for George Villiers,
Duke of Buckingham. It is still standing near the Thames Embank-
ment, at the end of Buckingham Street, Strand.

at Bloomsbury Square he was a regular worshipper at the Parish Church, of which the Rev. Montague Villiers was Rector. He used afterwards to say that the church was so full that only after two years' waiting could he obtain a sitting; and before that time he never sat down in the church, for if ever he got a seat in the aisle he had to give it up to some lady less fortunate.

His establishment at Bloomsbury Square was practically the commencement of business on his own account. During the first few years there were times indeed when work failed him, and his ardent spirit chafed against the oppression of enforced idleness, as will be seen from words written to his sister Mrs Wontner in 1846. "I am now again alone in the great city, and need some refreshment from the Provinces. Many and various are my schemes, and few of them do I seem to bring to bear; but I feel now I must rise up and act, and not sit dilly-dallying, conning them all over one after another. I am sadly too fond of day dreaming, and lately I have been very idle, seemingly without any fixed purpose of action. I suppose the true secret is want of sufficient work, and with this view I intend to undertake the illustration of another church, and publish it, pay or not pay; for idle and comfortable I cannot be, and it is better to do what does not help one onwards, than sit still and envy the busy people."

But it was not very long before the tide of

success began to flow. In the previous year, in spite of absence from home, his diary records that he had completed and delivered designs in four competitions. In 1843 the fruit began to appear. Hildenborough Church, "my first church won in competition," was the commencement. In the same year the restoration of Austrey Church, Warwickshire, became what he called "the first foundation-stone" of success. Four years later (1847) he competed for the restoration of the important Church of St Mary's, Scarborough. It was a bold venture, for men of note were in the field; and it brought out not only all his professional powers, but also that same undaunted resolution which he had shown at Leghorn. For he persisted in crossing from the Isle of Man, where he was staying, in the face of a stormy sea, and in spite of the urgent solicitations of his friends, in order that his designs might be delivered on the appointed day[1]. The result was felt to be a turning-point in his career. It brought him the warmest congratulations of his friends, and his own comment, written some years later, seems still to thrill with the elation of his first rise to distinction : " The corner-stone of success. The fruit of open competition...won by unanimous vote." After this he received (in 1850) the appointment to restore Wolverhampton Collegiate Church, "a fruit of the last-named

---

[1] The 'snowing up' described in his letter p. 33 seems to have belonged also to this journey.

(*i.e.* Scarborough), a work extended over 24 years."
Meanwhile the year of his success at Scarborough
had witnessed another recognition of his rising reputation, in his election to the office of Consulting
Architect to the Lichfield Diocesan Church Building
Society. It was his first unsolicited honour, of which,
though the remuneration was small, he was justly
proud, and for its timely encouragement, as well as
for the close connexion it brought with the See of
Lichfield and its occupants[1], he regarded it with
peculiar affection, and held it for nearly 50 years,
till his death. It bore moreover substantial fruit.
For this Lichfield appointment, following upon his
work at Scarborough, gained for him the important
distinction which he bore for the rest of his life, and
by which he became so widely known, of being appointed Architect to the Ecclesiastical Commissioners.

From a letter written in 1847 it appears that the
idea of marriage was beginning to exercise the
thoughts of his friends on his behalf, and possibly
also his own. At any rate on July 6, 1848, he
married Annie, daughter of Mr William Walker
Bentham, of Rochester, a kinsman of the celebrated Jeremy Bentham, and thenceforward he enjoyed for the rest of his days the peaceful joy of a
marriage assuredly made in Heaven. Shortly after
his marriage he took a small house, No. 6, Eton
Villas, in South Hampstead, thus beginning that con-

---

[1] Bishops Lonsdale, Selwyn and Maclagan.

nexion with the neighbourhood which ended only with his death. And in 1851, in consequence of his recent appointment as Architect to the Ecclesiastical Commissioners, he removed his office to No. 10, Whitehall Place[1].

From this point Mr Christian's life was one of quiet domestic happiness, and ceaseless labour—labour, however, which he supremely enjoyed, and which brought him a well-deserved reward of wealth sufficient for his wants and his liberality, of reputation, honourable position, and the esteem of valued friends. His work required him to spend many days each week in travelling about England. He estimated the total distance in one year at 27,000 miles. But travelling seemed to cause him no fatigue. By careful planning of his journeys, an art which he well understood, and was always ready to employ in the service of his friends, and by the happy gift which he possessed of being able to sleep soundly in the train, he was enabled to economize his strength. Economy of time was also effected by his practice of examining plans and writing letters and reports in railway carriages. These letters and reports, under whatever circumstances they were written, were always models of lucidity and careful accuracy. But in spite of all economies of strength and time, the office duties of his profession, involving the minute examination of designs and estimates, were laborious and exacting, and

[1] He removed finally to 8A, Whitehall Place, in 1861 or 1862.

left no space for leisure. In his earlier years he was frequently at work, as on his wedding day, before most men were about, and often continued until late at night. In his later years the Saturday 'half-holiday' was almost invariably so employed. On Sundays he scrupulously abstained from business, and gave his energy to the Sunday-school.

The progress of Mr Christian's professional career has been reviewed, by one better qualified to deal with it, in a separate chapter. In this therefore, which aims at sketching, however inadequately, the *home* life of the man, it is unnecessary to follow his career in detail, though a brief glance onward may be permitted at one or two incidents characteristic both of the architect and of the man. In 1861 the progress of the restoration of Chichester Cathedral, by Mr (afterwards Sir) Gilbert Scott, revealed the fact that the old Norman central tower, with its lofty spire, was in imminent peril of collapsing. Mr Christian, who had a reputation for judgment and experience in such matters, was at once called in to give his advice, and a day was fixed for his visit of inspection. By some accident however, as it might be called, his visit was postponed, and on that very day the tower suddenly fell. Happily it occurred at an hour when there was nobody in the building. But the inspection would probably have been going on at the time, and, by a devout mind, Mr Christian's absence could not but be regarded as an instance of that Providential care which he loved to recognize in the whole direction of his life, and to which he used humbly to attribute his preservation from all accident in the course of his many years of incessant travelling. The restoration of the cathedral was completed, and the tower and spire rebuilt by Sir Gilbert Scott. A similar catastrophe on a smaller scale was imminent, though happily averted, in the case of Alconbury Church, near Huntingdon, which was being restored by Mr Christian in 1876. The church possessed a tower of the thirteenth century, surmounted by an upper storey and a stone spire of the fourteenth. In the course of the restoration the lower storey of the tower showed ominous cracks, and other signs of giving way, so that the local builders were frightened and forsook the work. Mr Christian immediately called in a more experienced builder, and he used to tell how it came to him, as he lay awake one night, what plan he should adopt, and how the difficulties must be overcome. A huge framework of wood was constructed by which the upper storey was supported, as it were in the air[1], while the lower part was taken down and rebuilt on new foundations, until it could support the superstructure again. The work was, at the time, regarded as a triumph of hardihood and prompt resource. But it might hardly have been

---

[1] A brass tablet representing the tower in its state of suspension, was prepared by Mr Christian's direction, and set up in the church.

successful had not the Squire of the place, Mr George J. Rust, caught the enthusiasm of the architect, and given orders that no cost should be spared in giving effect to 'the baseless fabric of this vision.' Mr Christian assisted also in 1883 in preserving the tower of Norwich Cathedral, with its lofty stone spire of later date, from a similar fate, being consulted by the Dean and Chapter and their architect Mr Brown; he was consulted also in several other similar cases at different times. His restorations of Carlisle Cathedral and of Southwell Minster are alluded to on a later page. Thus Mr Christian's business continued to increase, and in course of time outgrew his own unaided powers. In 1875 he associated with himself his two partners, his cousin, Mr J. Henry Christian, and Mr Charles H. Purday, both of whom had for many years assisted him in his numerous works, and to whose valued co-operation he would have been the first to acknowledge his indebtedness.

With his settlement at Hampstead Mr Christian began that connexion with St John's (Episcopal) Chapel, Downshire Hill, to which he remained faithful all the rest of his life. Sunday after Sunday he was a regular worshipper in the congregation, and for 35 years he was constant to the duties of Teacher or Superintendent in the Sunday-school. Out of this connexion with St John's arose some of his most valued and lasting friendships.

In 1858 he removed with his wife and family of now three daughters to No. 3, Oak Villas, Haverstock Hill,—their home for the next 24 years. It was a home in which the sweet charities of the family circle spread out into wider sympathy with needs abroad. Thus began the interest which Mr Christian and his family thenceforward never ceased to feel in the neighbouring district of Gospel Oak, and in which they were constantly associated with their friends and neighbours, Mr and Mrs Robert Woodd. Gospel Oak was then in great part a benighted region of unfinished streets, muddy brickfields, and railway excavations, lying at the back of Haverstock Hill, in which the struggling energies of a newly-formed parish cried out for encouragement. Mrs Christian and Mrs Woodd opened the first schools and mothers' meetings. Mr Christian and Mr Woodd were always ready to further with advice and assistance every good undertaking. To the daughters of both families work amongst the poor of Gospel Oak became a kind of vocation. So the years went on. On June 25, 1872, Mr Christian's eldest daughter Eleanor was married to the Rev. Joseph Hargrove, and exchanged her home for the sphere of her husband's labours in the parishes successively of Gedling, Harpenden, Silsoe, and St Matthew's, Cambridge.

The other members of the family still maintained their interest in Gospel Oak. Encouraged by her father, Bessie, the second daughter, was instrumental in establishing the Rose and Thistle Coffee Tavern in 1879, and also gathered round her a large Men's Bible Class out of the same district. And it may here be added that some years later the connexion was drawn still closer by the marriage, in 1888, of this daughter with the Rev. George Cuthbert Blaxland, second Vicar of the parish. And when after a short married life she died on Jan. 1, 1890, Mr Christian's help was largely instrumental in the completion of a Mission Hall in which she had taken a keen interest, and in the erection of a Church Room to perpetuate her work and her memory.

For the recreation of his busy life Mr Christian desired little beside the quiet enjoyment of his home and the companionship of his wife and daughters. To this must, however, be added his autumn holiday. Waiting generally till September or October, for the sake of a meeting at Lichfield, and making many plans but adopting none till the last moment, he spent four or five weeks in travelling about Great Britain from Land's End to the Orkneys, or on the Continent, with a preference always for the sea, or for lofty situations and bracing air, no matter how cold. He was accompanied either by some member of his family or by some congenial friend. Into the enjoyment of these annual tours he threw himself with as much zest and energy as into his work ; and it was, doubtless, largely due to the refreshment derived from them, that he so long maintained unimpaired his faculties of mind and body. In 1874 when travelling on business, accompanied by Mrs Christian, he was suddenly seized with a virulent attack of erysipelas, which kept him prostrate for nine weeks in a hotel at Saltburn. But except for this illness his health was usually good, though symptoms of a weak heart from time to time caused him uneasiness. Erysipelas reappeared again fatally at the last.

Some extracts from letters written to his daughters at different times are here inserted. They show the writer as he was to those who knew him best,—keen in the enjoyment of life and activity ; ardent in his love of the beautiful and grand, whether in Nature or art ; tender in sympathy with little children, his own and others, whether adapting his words to their understandings or providing them with pleasures ; sympathetic too with dumb animals ; but wherever he was, always a lover of home—

"My heart untravelled fondly turns to thee."

The first two extracts are written from abroad to a little daughter aged successively five and eight, and have the freshness of sympathy with the mind of a little child.

THE GIANT HOTEL, COBLENZ,
Sept. 30*th,* 1860.

...My room looks out on to a very broad, beautiful river, across which there is a bridge made of boats tied together, and on each of these boats a fine flag has been flying all day in honour of the birthday of some great person. Such beautiful flags ! with all kinds of different animals painted on them. The river is called the Rhine, and it comes down from the mountains a long way off, and all sorts of boats and steamers sail upon it, up and down, up and down, all day long....Yesterday I was waiting at the side of another river, the Mosel, for another steamboat to bring me here, and as it was a long time coming, amused myself in talking to the little children on the shore—they could not understand what I said, but they laughed very much and I laughed too. I had a long time to wait, so I set to work and built them a church with some stones upon the sand, and put up a great stone with a sharp point as a steeple, and a little boy gave me a red apple to stick on the top of it, which I did, and stuck a quill tooth-pick into it as a spike. Then I levelled the sand all round, and put some stones on the outside to form the walls of the churchyard, and stuck in some smaller ones to represent grave-stones. I made it very complete, and the little children were very much amused by it.

GENOA, *Sept.* 24*th*, 1863.

...I and my four companions travelled over the mountains in a carriage with two horses, one of them called Nina, the other called Hans. Hans was a tall strong fellow who went straight on with his head right up, as much as to say, I can pull you up wherever you want to go. Nina was not so strong, and a little inclined to be lazy, so that the driver was always calling out "Nina! Nina! in avanti," which means *go ahead*, but Nina looked a nice little thing and gave a very affectionate glance every now and then to Hans, as much as to say, How good you are to help me, and how strong! But Hans kept his head straight on and trotted on nobly, and pulled us up to the top of the mountain, or rather those of us who chose to ride, but I walked and so did Mr Woodd: they had the assistance of another horse for the very steep part, a capital strong fellow, but I don't know his name. When we were up on the top of the mountains we saw in several places great masses of ice and snow not much higher up than ourselves, and the wind blowing over them was cold....We saw plenty of goats, some of them such pretty creatures! One with a fine beard came up to

Mr Teulon and me, and we plucked some green stuff, and it took it out of our hands and then let us stroke its back. In the afternoon when we passed, the *same* goat came out of the flock frolicking and skipping towards us as much as to say, I am very glad to see you again. Was not that funny? While we were on the hill the whole of the ground seemed alive with grasshoppers, they hopped and skipped and jumped about and made such a whirring with their wings!...On Monday Nina and Hans brought us down from the mountain in safety, and we bid them goodbye under a grape-vine, which was trained all over a lattice-work close to the inn, so as to make a green roof of vine leaves. ...In this place the streets are almost all paved with white marble, and there are strings of mules constantly going along, jingling the little bells which are fastened to their collars. You would be very much astonished to see them, they wear such great collars all covered with bright coloured stuffs and bells. They bring all sorts of things on their backs. Some are loaded with wood, some with wine casks, and jingle, jingle, jingle, on they always go.

The next extract shows the father in his home. Birthdays were always days of great observance among the young people of Oak Villas, and Mr Christian always chose his presents to them himself, sparing no pains to make them suitable.

8A, WHITEHALL PLACE,
April 15th, 1868.

...I have not bought you a book this time for a birthday present, but a picture; only I have not yet got it home. It is a lovely picture, one which I have often wished I could get for you, and now I hope I have secured a good one. It is so soft that it looks like velvet. Two little squirrels cracking nuts, and a sweet little bullfinch looking up at them from a twig, and piping with all his might. It is to be your own property but, like Mr Owl on the breakfast table, to remain in Mama's drawing-room...there it will be always to look at, for you and all the others, and I intend to have it nicely framed....I hope you have had a very happy day at Southboro'....Now that you have got into your teens you must try more than ever to advance in learning and knowledge, and wisdom which is the beginning of all true knowledge, and the beginning of that is the fear of the Lord. You must look in the Book of Proverbs and see what is said about wisdom, and read and remember it all your days. Goodbye, my dear child, may God's blessing be always with you and as you grow in years may you grow in grace like the blessed Jesus.

Home love breathes through all the details of the following description from Scotland with its vivid picture not only of the several features of the landscape, but also of the movements and even the dresses of the various actors in the scene. It was, moreover, always a pleasure to Mr Christian to note the simplicity and naturalness of the home life of persons in high position.

COUNTY SUTHERLAND,
EAST SEA COAST,
LATITUDE ABOUT 58°. 5'.
Sept. 30th, 1870.

...Whilst waiting for Mr Chalk to come down to breakfast, I take pen in hand this bright sunny morning to have a little talk with you. We left Inverness yesterday morning and came to Golspie, a pretty village on the coast of this county, in which is Dunrobin Castle, a splendid house like a French château, perched high above the sea-shore, but with terraces and woods and gardens all the way down to the shore. Such a magnificent house, and such beautiful gardens, I have not seen before in Scotland, and just now the Prince and Princess of Wales and all sorts of grand people are staying there, and to-day there is to be a grand review of the Volunteers. We walked through the gardens and on to the beautiful pasture which lies between them and the sand of the sea, and there I stayed to see the rifle shooting, where the Duke's eldest son the Marquis of Stafford, and his cousin and several noblemen and gentlemen were contending for the prize. Presently there came on to the ground a beautiful, light-coloured pony with baskets on each side of his back, covered with scarlet cloth, and in the baskets two little children in white dresses trimmed with black, and straw sailor hats with pink ribbons, and on another black pony a pretty little girl in light blue; the two first were the Princess's two youngest children, and the girl, Lady Alexandra Gower. Soon afterwards a lady drove a little basket carriage down with a Highland gentleman sitting with her; who she was I don't know, but presently afterwards the Princess of Wales and Duchess of Sutherland walked down and some more gentlemen, one of them leading the two elder princes in grey Highland dresses. They seemed very fond of him and he played all manner of tricks with them. Prince George climbed up on to his shoulders, and then he made the two hold on to his walking stick and he drew them up. The Princess got into the pony carriage for a seat and the Duchess sat down on the grass. The Princess had a nice brown silk dress (short), and the Duchess a black and white small check dress with pink ribbons and streamers. The Duke of Sutherland had a Highland dress of his own green and black plaid, but I should like you to have seen the rough dresses worn by the gentlemen in attendance. And the scene was so exquisitely beautiful, the fine expanse of grass near the sea, the beautiful hills and mountains stretching away to the westward of the Firth of Dornoch, the hill and park rising behind covered with most beautiful trees from bottom to top, then the lower garden stretching away for a quarter of a mile in beautiful colours with only a low grass bank between it and the field, then the great château rising up with many turrets and towers, standing out against the sky and clothed all round with trees of rich and varied colours, and the beautiful sky, and the calm sea, and the glorious sunlight, it was like a scene in fairyland! There!... When the Princess and Duchess and the little people left, I left too (5.30) and walked up to the hotel for dinner, and afterwards

we hired a small waggonette and in it with a pair of horses we
started on our north journey, and after two hours' drive arrived
at our resting-place. We are now on the road to Wick in
Caithness, and I am sitting in the carriage whilst the horses are
baiting.   There is a terrace in front of the little inn, and down
below it some 50 feet or more a rippling river sparkling in the
sunlight.   The sea is a very little way off and the air is fresh
and pleasant.   There are a lot of men in the house making a
prodigious gabbling in Gaelic, so that we almost seem to be in
a foreign land.   I shall probably send you a telegram to-morrow
which will announce the coming of this letter.   It is so pleasant
to let you all know where I am at the time when one is passing
through the country, that I cannot help enjoying the luxury now
that the post is so long in conveying letters.   I am just *now*
more than 700 miles from home, and to-morrow, at John o'
Groats, shall be 40 miles still further North.   Look at the map.
We are going on in the same carriage and with the same horses
all across the North of Scotland, and there is room for two little
people besides ourselves.   I heartily wish that you and Meg
could fly over and join us.

The extract which follows is interesting not only
for its own grace of description, but also for the
allusion to the difficulties which beset a former
memorable journey to Scarborough.   This journey,
which he tells us took place in 1847, was probably
that which laid for him ' the corner-stone of success.'

In the train, SCARBORO' STATION,
                    March 24th, 1871.
...Walking up the steep hill towards Hackness this morning
early, I pulled off the enclosed twig for you though I am afraid
it will not retain its beauty; it looked so lovely in the bright
morning glistening with mist drops!

I left York this morning before six, and was very glad of my
thick watchman's coat...   Now it is bright and *hot.*   Hackness
is *such a lovely* place, one of the most beautiful of its kind in

England. There are several valleys branching out in different directions, with banks and cliffs covered with wood of all kinds to enclose them, beautiful streams gurgling along in the bottoms, with stretches of fine grass on each side, and in the distance, though not very far off, wild heathery moors, making a rich purply-grey background to the view. If you could see this as I have twice seen it in the early mistiness of a bright frosty morning, you would be charmed and wild with delight; and I wish you could! I have been restoring a nice little church there which was founded before the Conquest. It stands so prettily with the road on one side and a brook on the other, dividing the church-yard from Sir Harcourt Johnstone's beautiful park, and its spire which is more than 600 years old, looks so pretty as you see it amongst the trees. I am now on my way to another church which is still older, and am just passing the station where I was snowed up more than 24 years ago, and had an army of 100 men to cut me out and get the train through to Scarborough. Fancy going 8 miles in 8 hours, with the snow on each side half-way up the carriage windows! But that is exactly how it was, and then fancy the delight of going out of the warm station-room at daybreak and plunging into the snow up to your neck by way of a wash: but that is exactly what I did, and I never enjoyed a bath so much before or since. You may fancy how I enjoyed my breakfast when I got it, and my dinner too 8 hours after, when I got at last into Scarborough after going 42 miles altogether in 23 hours and a half. How would you relish that? And yet I always think of it with delight, and have many reasons for remembering it besides that of passing the station just now.

Florence, visited in the autumn of the same year, exercised its wonted fascination over him, and its charm of natural beauty and of historical interest is thus not unworthily described:

ALASSIO, *Oct.* 31*st*, 1871.

I got your message at Genoa this morning and am minded

to send you a letter.... We have been travelling to-day from Genoa along one of the most beautiful roads in Italy called the Riviera, or sea-side road, and sometimes the Corniche or Cornice road, because it is carried along on the top of the rocks close over the sea, and sometimes 1600 feet above its level, rather higher than the great hill above Rydal and five times as high at least as Tintagel Head. So you may imagine how grand it is!... Our road to-day,—sometimes cut out of the rocks overhanging the Mediterranean, sometimes through grottoes or short tunnels cut through the rock, and when more inland bounded by olives and vineyards and orange groves and pines and figs and palms, and fringed with hedges of aloes, and with the deep blue waters dashing upon the rocks, or rolling upon the beach,—has been one constant succession of beautiful scenes.... Then we went on to Florence, or as it is called in Italian, Firenze or Fiorenze, meaning a city of flowers, one of the most beautiful cities in the world; in a most lovely situation on a plain watered by the river Arno, and bounded by hills and the more distant Apennines. A really charming spot, and within it has some splendid palaces, and a very fine Cathedral with a bell tower close to it, the highest and most beautifully enriched perhaps in the whole world. It was designed by Giotto, a famous artist of the 14th century, and he was told to build a tower higher and more beautifully enriched than any building of Greece or Rome, and he succeeded in his task.... There are some very beautiful gardens close to Florence, and the view from the heights beyond the city, at a place called San Miniato, where there is a very fine ancient church, is the most lovely I know. You see the whole city below you with the dome of its Cathedral, the finest in the world, Giotto's tower, the palaces, and the river running past them, and then the level plain stretching away to the mountains, so richly cultivated that you may see corn, wine and oil growing all together, the vines twining between the olive trees, and stretching from tree to tree in festoons, and the space between the olive trees filled with wheat or other such plants. Then on the hill opposite is Fiesole, where the famous astronomer and philosopher Galileo lived, and was visited by our poet Milton.... But I could go on all night telling you of the great men and wonderful treasures possessed by Florence, and you must not forget that the greatest poet of Italy, Dante, lived and was persecuted there, for it has been a city of cruelties as well as of beauties, and Savonarola, one of the greatest preachers who ever lived, was put to death there, because he told the truth and reproved the wickedness of the priests and people.

In 1879 Mr Christian extended his travels as far as to America. Starting early in September, the party, consisting of himself, with his daughters Bessie and Alice, and some friends, crossed to Quebec and made a tour through Montreal, Toronto, Niagara and Detroit to Chicago, including a *détour* to the White Mountains. From Chicago they returned viâ Cleveland, Philadelphia, and Boston, to New York. Mr Christian's letters are full of graphic descriptions of the enjoyment of the voyage, the keen air and the " grand waves, brilliantly lighted up by the sun, rushing past us in mighty volume, oh, so beautiful, so grand!"—of the glorious scenery on the Continent, especially of Niagara, and of the novelty, luxury and profuse magnificence of the cities. He was most impressed, perhaps, by the marble buildings of Philadelphia, and also by the Sunday-schools, " of magnificent dimensions," carried on by Mr Wanamaker in the same city. " There can be no doubt they do things grandly here, though mixed with a considerable amount of buncombe." He was much interested to notice at

Boston " that the Washington arms are quartered with the shield of the Christians."

The following characteristic account of his unpremeditated visit to Longfellow shall be given in his own words.

On our way to Auburn cemetery the coachman stopped at a nice old-fashioned wooden house in a beautiful garden, and told us it had been Washington's head-quarters in 1775, and was now the residence of the poet Longfellow. Another carriage drove up while we were there, and its occupants called : and our coachman wanted us to do the same, as he said Mr Longfellow was very glad to see strangers. However, our impudence was insufficient, and we drove on, and on the way voted that it would not do to call. However, as we came back, I plucked up courage to send in a card to ask permission to gather a few leaves in the garden, and the answer came out that Mr Longfellow would be very glad to see both myself and my daughters ; so in we all went and were most kindly received by the old gentleman, and left him quite delighted that we had made such a venture, which was pretty strong for three shy people ! The chair in which he sits was made out of the chestnut tree described in one of his poems about the blacksmith.

In the following year he was in Northern Italy, in the keen enjoyment of Verona and Venice.

In the train, TRENT TO INNSPRÜCK,
Oct. 27th, 1880.

...Now I must go back to Verona, which we left after dark last night, Verona la Degna, as it is justly called, for it is a beautiful city, beautifully situated at the foot of mountains, and with the Adige river and its snow waters rushing rapidly through it. It has always been an important city, and has had many worthy citizens, not omitting the poetical ones of

Shakespeare's creation. There is a fine photograph amongst mine at home of the tombs of the Scaligers, with the beautiful grilles of iron round them. Yesterday was fresh and beautiful, and we hâd seven good hours of seeing and walking, visiting the beautiful churches, and winding up with the great Roman amphitheatre, one of the most perfect now remaining...The Verona marble is of a rich red colour, and in the churches it is used in large blocks, some polished ; the interiors are very spacious, and the large and tall pillars look very fine and grand in their simple dignity. The great church of San Zeno has a grand tall tower of brick and marble, which was more than 100 years in building ; in the lower part it is quite plain, but at the top it has two tiers of belfry windows and a fine projecting cornice. There are two such towers in the city, the other being at the Municipal buildings, and more than 300 feet high. I can fancy what a fuss would be made in our country if an architect were to go on building quite plain for over 200 feet before he put in any ornament, except quite at the base ; people would say how bare and ugly it is, and yet these great architects knew what they were about, and everybody allows that the result is beautiful. They look so grand and dignified. I delight in them ! and all through North Italy the towers abound in the cities and in the plains, and on all the hill sides you see them shooting up into the sky and giving point and character to every landscape...

But now I must take you further back to Venice, which we sorrowfully left on Monday night after three fine days, including Sunday, spent on its waters. Our hotel was near the mouth of the Grand Canal, which our rooms, quite at the top of the house, each with its stone balcony, overlooked,—a charming position, such as I had never had in the old city before. It was delicious to walk out of the hall marble-paved, on to the steps going down into the lovely sea-green clear water, to get the fresh air before breakfast, and to step into our gondola afterwards. On Saturday and Sunday it was bright and clear and warm as in our July, but on Sunday afternoon there came a sudden storm of wind and thunder and lightning which swept up a great sea, and showed a different aspect of the place. But while the clouds were sweeping up there was a most magnificent sunset, and the contrast between the rich glow in the west and the dark rushing storm-clouds from the east, was something truly magnificent...The storm lowered the temperature some degrees, and brought us still clearer skies on the morrow, and such a sunrise! Right out of the sea it came with a sudden rush, lighting up the summits of the churches and palaces in the clear crisp morning air, and sending a glow of warmth over everything,—body and mind of the beholder included. Oh! it was beautiful, and that is another advantage of the October holiday, that you have, night and morning, such beautiful sights, and ample time between for all reasonable sightseers! Well, we have got into the city, but have as yet said nought of its delights. It is a great matter to be well housed by a sea-water canal in Venice, everything is so fresh and nice, and it is a delight simply to exist by the waterside with the fresh soft un-dusty air about you. I did enjoy it. But to San Marco—San Marco! What a glorious fane is that! You must not, if you wish to understand it, go and look at it like an ordinary church, but must go and *live* in it and read its mysteries slowly and laboriously, if you wish thoroughly to know and enjoy it; and this takes time and needs instruction, and Ruskin has very charitably reprinted those parts of his great book which relate to this church, and there is no guide like it. Without such guidance you may look at its mosaic-covered walls and say how beautiful this and that sparkling light is upon them, and how extraordinarily rich is the gold, and the time-coloured marbles of its walls and domes and floors, but you will go away without understanding the wonderful course of Scriptural teaching the pictures are intended to convey, or half the reasons, why in the ages long ago this great church was covered with such a grand pictorial history. And there, during the whole period of the rise and fall of the great republic, has the teaching been for all, rich and poor alike, who would care to read and understand it;

and it is very interesting to see all classes of people there, young and old, rich and poor, freely walking about and regarding it as their *home*, to enjoy its teaching or to worship at its altars; and throughout the church there is nothing of Mariolatry or superstition on its old walls, whatever there may have been introduced in more modern times...I do wish you could have been with me when I took my last look at the grand old front, lighted up by the last rays of afternoon sunlight. Not only the mosaics and the pictures, but the glass of the great west window glittered like burnished gold, and the whole Place of St Mark was brilliant in its effulgence... On Monday we went to see some very beautiful pictures which I had never before heard of; there is a small church called San Georgio, quite in a back part of the city, where the walls have all been painted by one of the greatest artists, Carpaccio by name; the church is only like a room of good size with a flat ceiling of timbers, and the pictures cover the whole surface of the walls in separate compartments; they represent St George conquering the Dragon and delivering the maidens, and scenes in the life of St Jerome,—a most wonderful series of subjects most beautifully treated; Ruskin has described them capitally, but the only place for reading what he has said, is in front of the pictures themselves, of which he brings out all the points.

In 1882 Mr Christian with his family moved from Oak Villas to the house which he had built for himself on the edge of the East Heath, Hampstead. Erected according to his own designs, by builders[1] in whom he had the fullest confidence, and growing up under the eyes of himself and family, the house may be said to have gratified his almost every wish, and to have been in many ways an embodiment of his own

---

[1] Messrs Cornish and Gaymer, of North Walsham.

character. The very walls and windows seem to utter
his thoughts, being adorned with inscriptions, under
the cornices of the chief rooms, round the outside,
and on the window-panes,—texts, mottoes, and verses
chosen with singular felicity from Holy Scripture
and his favourite authors.   There is not a chamber,
moreover, into which the sun does not at some time
shine.   The house was named Thwaitehead, after the
home of his mother's family in the beloved Lake
Country.   Here he settled down to enjoy in his latter
years, not rest, for that he desired not, but labour light-
ened by the assured position he had won. His health
was still vigorous, his faculties unimpaired, his con-
science clear, his home life unclouded. His friends,
moreover, were numerous and true. Here he attained
to one of the highest distinctions of his profession,
becoming President of the Royal Institute of British
Architects in 1884-6, and Gold Medallist in 1887.
Here some of his most responsible works were undertaken, *e.g.* the judgment of designs for Liverpool
Cathedral, and the survey of the City churches for
the Charity Commissioners.   Here he was called
upon by the munificent donor, then anonymous, to
design the National Portrait Gallery, which is probably the greatest, and likely to be the best known
of his works. No better estimate can, perhaps, be
given of his life and of the position to which he had
attained at this time, than that which is contained in
the modest yet dignified words in which he reviewed

his career, in a speech returning thanks for the gold medal of the " Institute," referred to above.

Mine has been a life of independent service, not of exploits. I have undoubtedly done much work, and some I hope of a valuable kind to those most interested; but I could not think of comparing myself with many of the men of mark who have preceded me in receiving this distinction; with the indomitable explorers, or the great architects and archæologists of our own and other countries; my highest ambition has been that of doing to the best of my ability the duty from time to time set before me to accomplish, and of maintaining unsullied, in every sense, the high character of an honourable and independent architect.

This medal, the gift, by their recommendation, of Her Most Gracious Majesty the Queen, I take to represent the general opinion of my brother architects that I have not been unsuccessful in attaining that end, and for that reason I accept, and must ever most highly value it, as the best reward, and greatest honour I could possibly desire, after a long career of professional labour. We most of us know what a laborious life is that of an architect; how numerous its risks, how many its disappointments, and although these are not unmixed with joys and delights of no ordinary kind, yet the burden is sometimes heavy, and the ordinary rewards hardly proportionate in value. At such times the possession of this visible token of your regard cannot fail to be cheering; and therefore, instead of regretting that it comes so late, I would rather rejoice that it has not reached me until the time when the evening light is approaching, and soothing thoughts are not unwelcome.

" The evening light is approaching "—it could not but be so. Mr Christian had now passed the 'threescore years and ten,' the ordinary lot of man. He had had in his earlier years to battle with many disadvantages. He had had experience that

"life hath room
For many blights, and many tears."

He had seen all his brothers and sisters pass away before him, and had keenly felt their loss. But he had had many blessings, uncertain though he knew well his tenure of them to be, and now while the 'labour and sorrow' of old age yet tarried, he still could, and did, enjoy to the full the health and happiness with which God had blessed him, especially the dear home ties which throughout his married life had remained unbroken. But the evening was approaching, and, with evening, also shadows. The first inroad into this citadel of his earthly happiness came with the death on Jan. 1, 1890, of his second daughter, Bessie, at the birth of her son, Mr Christian's only grandson. It brought a dark cloud over a family that had not experienced bereavement before, and Mr Christian felt it deeply, though silently. He had secretly vowed to complete the Mission Hall, mentioned on an earlier page, as a thank-offering, if it should please God to restore his beloved daughter from the gates of the grave. And accepting with a heavy heart, but in humble submission, the issue which was good in the sight of God, he still carried out his purpose as a memorial of her whose desire was thus accomplished, though she lived not to see it. He still kept up his habits of assiduous labour, and of needful recreation. In the spring of 1890 he travelled to Italy to meet his old friend Prof. Hayter Lewis, and his son-in-law, the Rev. G. C. Blaxland, returning from the East, and found something of his old delight in retracing the steps of his early travel, Naples, Pompeii, Amalfi and Rome, with his old travelling companion. In the autumn of the same year he paid a visit to his beloved Lake Country, with his wife and younger daughters; and by a happy coincidence his eldest daughter, with her husband and children, was near by, so that for a week the now narrowed family circle was complete in a place which was hardly less dear to each than Hampstead itself. The cherished memory of those days has been recorded by one of the party—

" From the Ferry Hotel on the banks of Windermere they took long drives, the old man delighting to revive memories of the past, and to revisit scenes familiar to his youth. The school at Hawkshead, where his father had sat side by side with Wordsworth; his grandmother's tomb at Rusland, and that of the old Vicar of Crossthwaite,—husband of three wives, of whom the two later were laid in a tomb separate, though of equal dignity, while he lay down to rest with the first,—all were revisited, and care taken that any needed repairs should be done to each. But it was apparent to all that the deep shadow of the sad New Year's Day was upon his spirit, and that though he said no word of it, he was bidding a long farewell to scenes endeared to his heart by ancient family ties, and by the memory of many happy days, as well as by their own loveliness."

In the autumn of 1892 however, and also of 1893,

he made acquaintance with the fiords of Norway, voyaging in the "Victoria" with parties of congenial friends. And in the following year, 1894, he went for a short holiday to the South of France with Mr W. Harris. It was to be his last tour. But his letters still show the same keenness of observation and interest, and clearness of description as of old.

ST JEAN DE LUZ, HOTEL DE FRANCE.
18/10/94.

...As I have been buying a scarlet cap (Spanish, from Tolosa) for Christopher, I send you a line or two of thanks for your last cards, which I greatly appreciated....This day we have taken an open victoria to come to this place, 9 miles from Biarritz, and the drive was very refreshing. This is getting quite close to the Pyrenees, of which we can see some minor points of no great height; to-morrow we hope to get closer, and to see St Sebastian and Fuentarabia....This is a nice little town....There is here, what is very interesting to me, a large church; simple nave, 60 feet wide, and 125 feet long up to the transepts, and probably at least 60 feet beyond, with small transepts and chancel, the walls of the latter literally covered with niches and statues painted and gilded, but hard to discern. A very fine model of a church for a great preacher. But another peculiarity is that there are three stories of galleries made of timber with open fronts, only wide enough for a single row of seats in each, and not at all obtrusive. A large organ occupies the western end, and, if filled, such a church would be a splendid spectacle. Oddly enough, this is roofed in the same way as that I am building at Stoke Newington, and there was a church at Poitiers on the same simple plan almost identical in idea with mine, which has a triple arch at the east end. My church is to be consecrated next month, and you must go and see it. Only of course, my church, which will cost less than £9000, cannot compete with such monsters as those of the 12th and 14th centuries....I wish I could find a photograph of oxen dragging carts from church for Christopher, but have so far not seen one. I must write him a letter as soon as I can, but I also want to write to other small folk, and have but small chance of doing it, except as I am doing this, by picking up the fragments of time as I go ; so I always carry my letter-case with me, sometimes fruitlessly, often usefully.

Mr Christian was never the same man again after the sorrow of 1890, and had to acknowledge a sense of the growing infirmity of age. There was indeed no warning of rapid decay. In February, 1895, in his eighty-first year, he could still climb a ladder with many a younger man, and was most unwilling to relax any of his habits of work. But the energy to resist or shake off an attack of illness was failing.

The end came suddenly. On Saturday, Feb. 16th, 1895, while iron-bound frost lay on the land, and the east wind of a prolonged winter blew chill and keen, he paid a visit to a friend, and on leaving was seen to shiver as he wrapped his overcoat around him. The next day he was unwell. Erysipelas soon disclosed itself, and after four days of painless, because unconscious, illness, on the morning of Thursday, February 21st, he breathed his last. With what feelings of startled sorrow the news was heard among his many friends, especially of Hampstead, has been touchingly told in the preface to this sketch. For the 'sadness of farewell' to those who were closest and dearest there are no words. But to grief, even the deepest, staying itself in Christian Faith upon the comfort of 'a voice from heaven,' it is often given to find cause even for thankfulness in the manner of its visitation. So now to those who mourn in Mr Christian a husband, father, friend, it is given to be thankful for his long and noble life, to which death brought swift release from present suffering and from the fear of lasting consequences. He came to his grave 'in a full age, like as a shock of corn cometh in, in his season.' No narrowing of the full stream of his life into contracted channels, no trial of long-continued sickness or of enfeebled powers, sadden the memory of one who, 'after he had served his own generation by the will of God,' thus ' fell on sleep.'

The funeral service was held on Monday, Feb. 25th, in St John's Chapel, Downshire Hill, where for 45 years he had worshipped in simplicity, and his body was laid to rest in Hampstead Cemetery, by the side of his daughter. The spot is marked by a plain granite slab, signed with the Cross, and bearing the following inscription :—

IN REVERENT AND LOVING MEMORY OF
EWAN CHRISTIAN, ARCHITECT,
SEPT. 2o, 1814—FEBY. 21, 1895.
WITH GOOD WILL DOING SERVICE AS TO THE LORD AND NOT
TO MEN.

That I may win Christ, and be found in Him, not having mine own righteousness...but that which is through the faith of Christ.
SALUS PER CHRISTUM : TRUST AND STRIVE.

IN THE SUNDAY SCHOOL.

The following notice of Mr Christian's Sunday-School work has been written for this book by the Rev. J. Kirkman, Vicar of St Stephen's, and formerly Incumbent of St John's Chapel, Hampstead.

Mr Christian was Superintendent of the Downshire Hill Sunday-school for upwards of 35 years. His devotedness to the work was a very strong feature in his character. It was his constant rule, hardly ever broken, to return home from any distance on Saturday evening, that he might be at his post and in Chapel on Sunday. His extreme regularity was most remarkable in a gentleman so incessantly occupied with important work during the week. And

this served as an irresistible example for the Teachers.
He was particularly punctilious about the marking of
the attendance Register, as to Teachers as well as
children. Whenever not actually engaged in marking,
or in visiting the classes, he was reading the " Teacher's
Bible," standing at the desk. He would never sit down.
In later years, although feeling the work and the
contact with boys somewhat of an effort, he was but
very gradually persuaded to resign. I could never
arrive at any precise reason why he carved the curious
motto over the new wooden architrave of the fire-
place, "A tale-bearer revealeth secrets : " and another,
" Where no wood (fuel) is, the fire goeth out; so where
no tale-bearer, the strife ceaseth." I considered
them characteristic of his severe integrity, and noble-
ness of disposition.

Two of our red-letter days worth remembering
were his silver wedding-day, on which he took all
the children and Teachers to Bushey Park, and feasted
us handsomely : and the great centenary gathering,
of all London Sunday-schools, in the grounds of
Lambeth Palace, in 1880.

The following are entries in our Register-book :

On the title-page—in his writing :

" In quietness and confidence shall be your
strength."

*Here are two pages opposite each other : one in his
handwriting : the second in mine :*

"A blank page to record a blank in the old
Sunday School.
George Edward Smith, for 57 years
a teacher in Downshire Hill School :
died, 1 January, 1889.
Eheu !
Blessed are the dead which die in the Lord.
Yea, saith the Spirit, that they may rest from
their labours : and their works do follow them.
Amen.
Zeal. Constancy. Perseverance. Truthfulness. Love.
A bright example of a faithful servant
of the Master."

"A blank page to record another blank in the
Old Sunday School.
Ewan Christian, for 30 years Teacher and
Superintendent in Downshire Hill Sunday School,
Died 21 February 1895 : aged 80 years.
We shall not look upon his like again.
Know ye not that there is a prince and a great
man fallen this day in Israel ?   2 Sam: 3: 38.
Well done, good and faithful servant, enter thou
into the joy of thy Lord.   Matt: 25: 21.

The opposite page is in his handwriting.
Earnestness : strictness : constancy : sincerity :
love of his Bible : doing all, secular and sacred, as
Architect or Teacher, in the name of the Lord Jesus."

In connexion with S. Stephen's Church may be mentioned his cordial determination and influence to maintain a kindly Christian good-feeling between the newly-created Parish Church and S. John's Chapel. His great interest in the building had much influence in various respects upon our architect Mr S. S. Teulon. He was urged to undertake the position of architect, but retired in Mr Teulon's favour. He insisted strongly upon a tremendous excess of concrete *foundation* for the east end of the Church. This exactly indicates his character: severe integrity and thoroughness: and a *good foundation* in all things small and great, temporal and spiritual. He was very strong in the particulars of plenty of *light*, and abundance of air and ventilation, and wide freedom of ingress and egress. I never knew a man who took more sympathetic judicious views of beauty, and harmony, in form colour, proportion: and even so also in literature and all art, as well as his own speciality.

His particular gifts to St Stephen's Church were the sturdy *font*, with its beautiful marble central and side shafts; and the most charming one, in a pleasing simple design, free of demonstrativeness, of all the capitals of the pillars of the nave, with a mosaic disc above, inclosing a likeness of Bishop Latimer.

I never conversed with him without learning something from him, and *feeling stronger* because of my contact with him. I invariably had this feeling over me. I cannot remember that, in my humble opinion on any subject, practical or speculative, I could ever differ from him in a matter of judgment. He knew well how greatly I appreciated him.

CHAPTER II.

WORK.

Friend to truth, of soul sincere,
In action faithful, and in honour clear;
Who broke no promise, served no private end,
Who gained no title, and who lost no friend.

POPE.

THE passing away from among us, full of years and honours, of a man so distinguished in the profession as Ewan Christian[1], deserves to be recorded fully, and his professional career traced systematically, while the recollections of his strong personality and his skill as an architect are fresh in our memory. Over fourscore years at the time of his death, age had not dimmed his eyesight nor impaired his judgment. Active and vigorous to the last, there were none of those symptoms which we look upon as inseparably connected with old age, when men arrive at that limit when their "strength is but labour and

---

[1] This notice was written for the *Journal of the Royal Institute of British Architects* by Mr George H. Birch, F.S.A., Associate R.I.B.A., Curator of the Soane Museum. The author has since kindly corrected and enlarged it for this memoir.

sorrow." Of him it might be truly said, " He died in harness"; like Edward Barry, George Edmund Street, and William Burges, called away when the productions of their graceful fancy were being realized ; and yet unlike them in one respect, for while they were removed in the vigour and prime of life, Ewan Christian had passed the allotted term and was still at work.

His early years were passed at Christ's Hospital, and it may be that he owed much of his good health and freedom from fatigue in after life, and his active and strong disposition, to the healthy surroundings, the open-air life, and almost Spartan fare of the school in those days. In every sense he remained an " old Blue " to the end of his days, always speaking of his school with affection, ever ready to help those who required his help and whom he had known in former years. He became a Governor afterwards, and up to the very last assisted the governing body of the Institution with his sound advice and mature judgment, in the vexed question of the proposed removal to some place far distant from its old associations and historic site, on account of the parrot-like cry of " insanitary surroundings."

After leaving school he was articled to Matthew Habershon, in whose office he was distinguished both for his industry and zeal in acquiring a knowledge of his profession. From Habershon's office he passed to that of Brown of Norwich, who was surveyor to the Cathedral. Returning to London, he was for some time with Mr Railton, with whom he worked on one of the competition sets of drawings for the Houses of Parliament—the busy record of a busy period. His close application to work injured his eyesight, and it became absolutely necessary for him to abandon for the time all fine drawing; so he became a clerk of works, and superintended the progress of several buildings, especially St Margaret's, Lee (which, since then, has been largely altered and transformed by Mr James Brooks), and the large Union at Colchester. At this period he was also helping Habershon, and making sketches for his work[1] on half-timbered houses. All this varied ex-

---

[1] *The Ancient Half-Timbered Houses of England,* by MATTHEW HABERSHON, Architect, London, 1836. The author states in his Preface that "the specimens which he obtained were in the first instance almost exclusively limited to the County of Worcester, and the more immediate neighbourhood of Droitwich. Having however obtained information that there were some remarkably fine ones in other places, particularly in Lancashire and Cheshire, he sent one of his pupils, Mr Ewan Christian, to try to find them out and sketch them. The result of this journey far surpassed his expectation, and produced the most ample and beautiful materials for the completion of the work." Mr Christian's commission seems however to have extended to Shropshire also, and eleven of the eighteen large lithographs in the book are from his sketches. The subjects of these are an old House in the Market Place, Preston; the Hall i' the Wood, near Bolton; Samlesbury Old Hall, and Ince Hall, Wigan—all in Lancashire; Bramall Hall (two) and Moreton Hall in Cheshire; and in Shropshire, Pitchford Hall; an old House in Butchers' Row, Shrewsbury, and Park Hall, Oswestry. He contributed also a view of an old house in Hereford, and some measured drawings of architectural details. All these are most interesting, both as views of some of the most picturesque old houses

perience, undertaken and carried through with that devotion to duty, that minute attention to all small details and complete mastery of them, which eminently distinguished him in whatever he undertook, made his advice and guidance in after life so valuable to those who had to submit to him in his official capacity the drawings and specifications of any building. His reports as a clerk of works were perfect models in their way; nothing was forgotten or unrecorded, and no defect was unnoticed. Strictly true and upright himself, he looked for the same in others, and woe betide them if they were found wanting!

In 1841—42 he went abroad, studying for a time in Italy, where he made acquaintance with (Sir) Horace Jones, and Arthur Green, both of whom died before him, and Professor Hayter Lewis, happily still surviving. Very beautiful and accurate were some of the sketches he made. The writer remembers on one occasion being shown a minute sketch of some lovely Italian work, which he took for a print. "Print! no print—look again; you should use your eyes as I did when I made the sketch." It would astonish a good many to see these sketches, and contrast them with the "scratch and splash" style of the present day.

On his return he commenced practice, taking part in several competitions, many of which he gained.

in England, and as specimens of Mr Christian's wonderful skill and accuracy in architectural drawing.

About this time he built his first Church at Hildenborough, near Tonbridge. The restoration of the old
church of St Mary, Scarborough, was the result of a
competition in which he was successful. From that
time his position as an architect was assured, and
his works followed in rapid succession. His earliest
Churches, such as Hildenborough and St Stephen's,
Tonbridge, show a distinct advance on the usual
style of that period, although they may fall short
of the high standard of the ultra-correct ideal of the
Ecclesiologist. He had a thorough knowledge of old
work, and how carefully he had studied it is ex-
emplified in his *Architectural Illustrations of Skelton
Church*[1],—the only *book* which he ever published,
although several of his reports on Churches were
printed in pamphlet form, and many of his addresses
and remarks in the course of discussions are to be
found in the volumes of the R. I. B. A. Journal.

He had become a student of the Royal Academy
early in the "thirties," and must necessarily have
attended the lectures on architecture given by the
then Professor of Architecture, Sir John Soane, with
whose works he could have had but little sympathy.

[1] This is a monograph on an exceedingly interesting Church of
the first half of the 13th century, evidently by the hands of the same
masons who had worked on York Minster, a building of the same
period. The author alludes to a tradition current in the parish that the
Church was built with the stones that remained over after the South
Transept of the Minster was finished. The volume contains views of
the exterior and interior, with carefully measured drawings, and descriptive letter-press. Skelton is about four miles from York.

A fellow-student[1], older than Ewan Christian, still alive and hearty, who well remembers him, and who only recently renewed an acquaintance first formed sixty years before, when telling the writer of his interview, said, " I found him just as enthusiastic in manner " and conversation as he was sixty years ago."

His first drawing exhibited at the Royal Academy was in 1833, and was probably an Academic one, as it is called in the catalogue a " Design for a Mausoleum," and the address given is 61 Mortimer Street, Cavendish Square, which was Mr Habershon's office. He was then in his 19th year, and in the third year of his articles, and from that time until 1855 he contributed some sixteen drawings, but not annually. After that date comes a long interval, and it is not until 1874 that he is again represented on the walls of the Academy, this time with three drawings. The last time he exhibited was in 1879. Appended is a tabulated list of the subjects which he exhibited :

1833.   Design for a Mausoleum.

1834.   Design for a Lodge and Park Entrance to a Nobleman's Mansion.

1835.   Design for a New Church to be erected at Kendal.

1843.   South-east view of the New Church at Hildenborough, Kent.

[1] Mr John Green Waller, F.S.A.

1846. South door at Skelton Church.
Proposed Church at Pembury, Kent.

1847. Design for New Offices for the Imperial Assurance Company. (Competition Drawing, 2nd premium.)

1848. Church of St Mary, Scarborough.

1850. New Church, Wickham Bishops.
Abnalls, Lichfield.

1851. Interior of Church—Wickham Bishops.

1854. Interior of St Luke's, Nutford Place.

1855. Collegiate Church of St Peter, Wolverhampton.
Interior of Choir, Carlisle Cathedral.

1874. Highlands, Gloucestershire—two views.
St Mark's, Leicester.

1879. Glyndebourne, Sussex.

It would be a long record to give his works in their successive order, the bare list of Churches, Episcopal and Capitular residences, Rectories, Vicarages, Schools, private mansions, and houses of business, which he had built, restored or enlarged, filling many folio pages. Of these some of the more important are enumerated at the end of this chapter, but we may here offer some brief comments upon a few of those of chief interest. Among these was Carlisle Cathedral, then in a terrible state of disrepair; its choir had been covered with a plaster vault, which he removed, opening out the old oaken roof above;

and subsequently he had to clear out and repair the transepts and the only surviving bays of the nave. The Collegiate Church of St Peter, Wolverhampton, being much decayed from the soft nature of the red sandstone of which it was built, was substantially repaired by him ; while a ruinous chancel, which had usurped the place of the old one, was entirely rebuilt; and so conservative was he, that he rebuilt it as a long collegiate chancel, although the Deanery of Wolverhampton had for years ceased to exist. Another careful 'restoration,' in the best sense of the word, was the fine old Minster at Southwell, now a Cathedral Church. As an instance of his extreme carefulness, it may be mentioned that when it was a question of rebuilding the leaden spires which once adorned it, he came across a sketch by J. M. W. Turner, R.A., showing these spires ; he resolved to follow that sketch, rather than make them higher—which. many would have preferred—"because," he said, "Turner was always "correct in his architectural drawings, and he sketched "those spires as he saw them, and as they undoubt-"edly existed."

He was not yet forty when he became Consulting Architect to the Ecclesiastical Commissioners—a most important appointment, though not a very enviable one, it being incumbent upon every architect to send in for his approval drawings and specifications of every Church intended for a district Church, and of every house proposed to be conveyed to the

Commissioners for a Parsonage. On these drawings he had to sit in judgment, and sometimes, unfortunately, very severe judgment; confining himself, however, principally to details of construction and plan, and never interfering much with the design, unless money were absolutely wasted on unnecessary ornament. Some of his professional brethren may have thought him exacting and capricious; but he was always just, and his requirements were invariably dictated by sound common sense. No one could have filled that position better than he did, "without fear or favour"; whether the drawings before him were the works of an intimate friend[1] or a perfect stranger, it was precisely the same to him; he had a duty to perform to the Commissioners, and he did it.

With regard to the churches and parsonages which he built for the Commissioners, for which they found all the funds, the same rule which he applied to others he applied to himself; he would rather spend money on sound work and solid foundations which did not show, than on external showi-

---

[1] In illustration of this absolute impartiality, we may quote some words from a letter of (probably) his oldest surviving friend, Mr Thomas C. Hine, of Nottingham, Architect. Speaking of his "rigid adherence to what he believed was just and right," he adds, "This characterized his decision in an Architectural Competition in which I was concerned, and when I was deluded enough to think that if I came anywhere *near* the mark, his affection for an old friend would induce him to yield a point—but no, had I come only within one mark of what he deemed to be the best design, it would have failed, and it would have been vain to expect the slightest concession for friendship's sake."

ness of detail and ornament, which might have made his buildings more attractive, but at the expense of, solidity. His hatred of all shams in architecture was proverbial; his church work was invariably honest and sound, and never in a single instance flimsy or unsubstantial. During the long period of forty-four years that he served the Commissioners he built many large and fine churches, which are distinguished more for their quietness and repose than for architectural effect, although they are by no means wanting in that. One of his finest and best churches, built by private munificence, was St Mark's, Leicester. Among other ecclesiastical buildings the group of houses for the Minor Canons of St Paul's, which form a little Cathedral-close in themselves, with an entrance under an archway from Warwick Lane, deserves more than passing mention.

His domestic works were also very numerous, including many large mansions and manor houses. In all these there is the same feeling displayed— quiet repose, no straining after picturesque effects, genuinely English in character, with many mullioned windows and tall chimneys and red-brick gables, carrying on the tradition of the "stately homes of England," except in neighbourhoods where stone was procurable, for he never neglected local material.

In London his architectural taste and genius are apparent in a building for the Economic Life Assurance Society, Bridge Street, Blackfriars, a façade where for once he allowed the results of his Italian studies of brick and terra-cotta to be utilized ; though he reverted again to a more English type for the façade of Messrs Cox's Bank at Charing Cross. The last in the long list of his works is one virtually completed externally, and only lacking a few fittings internally, but which, alas ! he was not permitted to see finished—the National Portrait Gallery. In this building there were difficulties to be overcome, and one may hope for a favourable verdict, when the hoardings are all cleared away, that he did successfully meet those difficulties. There was the existing National Gallery, with its returned front facing St Martin's Church, and this Neo-Græco work of Wilkins' poor commonplace design—not so much the fault of Wilkins, but arising more from the fact of his having to use up the front of Carlton House, and the proportion of the Order used there regulating the proportions of his building. Now, again, this in its turn has influenced Mr Christian's design, for in the new National Portrait Gallery this work of Wilkins had to be continued and harmonized, and it is not until one arrives at the corner, where that work could be shut out, that he had a free hand. Here he entirely departed from a style of architecture forced upon him by the exigencies of the case in having to complete Wilkins' returned front, and adopted a free rendering of early Florentine work, such as one would see at the Palazzi Strozzi or Medici. The result is a building distinguished for its repose and dignity, and one which could not be mistaken for anything else but that for which it was designed—a Picture Gallery, and a Gallery worthy of the long roll of national celebrities whose portraits are to be preserved within its walls.

In addition to the post of Consulting Architect to the Ecclesiastical Commissioners, he was also Consulting Architect to the Lichfield Diocesan Church Building Society and to the Carlisle Diocesan Society, and was one of the architects of the Incorporated Church Building Society—all three, however, honorary appointments. In 1887 (in consequence of the passing of the " City of London Parochial Charities Act" 1883), he was appointed Consulting Architect to the Charity Commissioners, in whom were vested all the funds derived from the various charities connected with the old Parish Churches in the City. In this capacity he had to visit and report on the actual state of each church, and what sum of money was necessary, not only for the repairs then needed, but also to keep them annually in repair. Every report was accompanied with a plan of the church and a detailed estimate of repairs ; and this series of reports, forming the most complete account of the City Churches ever written, is a monument in itself to his untiring zeal and business capacity.

In later years his wide experience and mature judgment were frequently in demand for judging

competitive plans for ecclesiastical and other buildings. Among the more important of such competitions were those for the Cathedrals of Edinburgh and
Liverpool; the new Admiralty[1] and War Offices; the
Training College at Norwich, and the new buildings
for Christ's Hospital at Horsham, a subject to which
he devoted much thought and grateful care, and for
which he received a special vote of thanks[2] from
the Governors. His report on the designs for Edinburgh Cathedral was considered a model of fairness
and lucidity.

He was one of the oldest members of the Institute,
for he was made an Associate in 1840[3], became a
Fellow in 1850, Vice-President, and President in
1884—1886. During his presidency the Institute
celebrated its Jubilee. In 1887 he was the recipient
of the Royal Gold Medal.

His striking personality was remarkable; to many
he might have appeared grim and unapproachable,
but under that somewhat stern exterior there lurked
the kindliest and best of natures and warmest of
hearts. Once strike a chord and the whole nature of

[1] The recently erected Admiralty is not however from the design to
which he gave the preference.

[2] By a singular coincidence the letter conveying their thanks is
dated on the 71st anniversary of his admission to the school, June 11,
1823.

[3] In the R.I.B.A. Kalendar for 1894—5, his name is *fourth* in
seniority among the 617 Fellows; those of earlier date being James
Piers St Aubyn (1837), Henry Clutton (1838), and David Brandon
(1839).

the man awoke in responsive echo; he would be carried away by enthusiasm, scarcely finding words to express the fulness of his heart. Boundless in his charity, many a recipient of that bounty will feel his loss. To those in his employ he was ever a kind and generous master; a terror to wrongdoers, from that impatience of wrong which was so characteristic of him, yet withal he could be patient and forgiving. Of his private life it does not become one to speak, for "through all the track of years he wore the white "flower of a blameless life." But in his public capacity we never shall look upon his like again. Indeed, we can ill spare him, and his closing words in his Opening Address to the Institute in 1884 read like a legacy to his professional brethren:—"We have seen, I think, "that the aim of the Founders of this Institute was "high and noble; let our standard in the future be "raised still higher. Their work was begun in weak-"ness, let ours be continued in strength; and, putting "aside all petty jealousies, let us combine not for mere "personal advantage, but in the truest and most "liberal sense, for the advancement of our art, and "the establishment of its practice on that broad basis "of honourable principle which alone is worthy of the "noble profession to which we belong." This was no empty sentiment, but the guiding principle on which he acted throughout his professional life.

The following is a list of some of the most important works executed by Mr Christian.

NEW CHURCHES.

1844. St John's, Hildenborough[1].

1849. St Thomas', Douglas, Isle of Man.

1851. Christ Church, Forest Hill[1].

1852. St Stephen's, Tonbridge[1].

1852. St John's, Kenilworth.

1855. St Luke's, Nutford Place[1].

1859. St Peter's, Rochester[1].

1860. Christ Church, Winchester.

1860. St Peter's, Hamsey.

1861. St Stephen's, Spitalfields.

1862. St James', Tunbridge Wells.

1868. St Mary's, Carlisle.

1868–89. Holy Trinity, Folkestone.

1871. St Benet's, Stepney.

1872. St Mark's, Leicester.

1873. St Mary's, Hoxton.

1874. All Hallows, Bromley-by-Bow.

1874. Christ Church, Weymouth.

1875. St Paul's, Clerkenwell.

1876–89. Holy Trinity, Scarborough.

1877. Christ Church, Stepney.

1878. St Antholin's, Nunhead.

1879. St Matthew's, Cheltenham.

1879. St Anthony's, Stepney.

[1] These were won in competition.

1879. Holy Trinity, Dalston.

1880. St Stephen's, Upper Holloway.

1885. St Barnabas, Kentish Town.

1885. St Dionis, Fulham.

1885. St Peter's, Limehouse.

1885–90. St Paul's, Longridge.

1889. St Thomas, Finsbury Park.

1894. St Olave's, Stoke Newington.

CHURCHES RESTORED.

Carlisle Cathedral.

Southwell Minster.

Romsey Abbey (Chancel).

St Mary's, Scarborough[1].

St Peter's, Wolverhampton.

And the following Parish Churches :

Nuneaton, Coggeshall, Holbeach, Knaresborough, East Meon, Prittlewell, Bampton, Dersingham, Castle-acre, Bosham, Eastbourne, Tonbridge, Kempsey, Alconbury, Skelton[2] (near York), Margate, St Mary's, Cheltenham Minster (Sheppey), Tong, St Cuthbert's, Wells ; and about 150 others in all parts of England and Wales, in addition to the repairs to Churches and Chancels, about 200 in all, done for the Ecclesiastical Commissioners.

In the City of London a complete survey made for the Charity Commissioners of 54 Churches, with

---

[1] Won in competition.

[2] Note by Mr Christian. "Restored 40 years after E. C. had published his book on it " (see p. 56).

reports as to general condition, repairs then needed and provision for future maintenance. Also the restoration of the following :

St Andrew Undershaft.

Sts Anne and Agnes, Gresham Street.

St Olave's, Hart Street.

St Botolph's, Aldersgate.

St Michael's, Paternoster Royal, Castle Hill.

St Martin's, Ludgate.

Episcopal Residences.

Norwich and Gloucester, almost entirely rebuilt, and works of addition or restoration at Lambeth, Bishopsthorpe, Lincoln, and new Chapels added at Llandaff and Manchester.

Capitular Residences.

St Paul's—six Minor Canonries and Gatehouse (built).

Westminster Abbey—Choir House (built).

Bangor—Canonry (built).

Chichester—Canons' Gate (restored).

Exeter—the Chantry (built).

Llandaff—Deanery, Canonry, and Minor Canonries (built).

St Asaph—Canonry (built).

Wells—Chain Gate (restored).

Other Ecclesiastical Buildings.

Rectories, Vicarages, Parsonages and Curates' Houses, about 200 in all, varying in cost from £800 to £4000, in almost every County in England and Wales; some built for the Ecclesiastical Commissioners, others for private patrons. Also Mission Halls, Parish Rooms and Vestries; National and Parochial Schools, about 20 in number, including the Cathedral Grammar School, Worcester.

Other Buildings.

St John's College, Highbury—Chapel, Hall, Gateway and other additions; St Andrew's Convalescent Home, Folkestone, with large Chapel; Surrey Convalescent Home, Seaford; Economic Life Assurance Office, Blackfriars; Cox's Bank, Charing Cross; Whitaker's Works, Warwick Lane; McCorquodale's Printing Works, Southwark; and his last and greatest work, the National Portrait Gallery, which he did not live to see quite completed.

Mansions and Country Houses built.

1862. Lavington Manor, Wilts. Rt. Hon. E. P. Bouverie.

1864-8. Ascot Wood, Berks. Sir John Shaw Lefevre.

1862–9.	Coombe Warren, Surrey. Henry B. Mildmay, Esq.
1862–4.	Woodlands, Hampstead. Robert B. Woodd, Esq.
1865–70.	Abbotswood, Gloucestershire. Alfred Sartoris, Esq.
1865–68.	Frognal, Sunningdale. Admiral Sir Frederick Grey.
1867–70.	Foscott Manor, Buckingham. Captain L. R. Hall.
1870–75.	Highlands, Gloucestershire. Mrs Frith.
1852.	Oxley Manor, Wolverhampton. Alex. Hordern, Esq.
1862–64.	Loughrigg Brow, Ambleside. Rev. Canon Bell.
1874–78.	Eastbury Manor, Surrey. General Hagart.
1876–82.	Broadwell Hill, Moreton-in-the-Marsh. Piers Thursby, Esq.
1880–85.	Lillingstone Dayrell, Bucks. Abraham John Robartes, Esq.
1882–86.	Holbrook Hall, Suffolk. J. Mitchell, Esq.
1883–87.	Bosahan, Cornwall. A. P. Vivian, Esq.
1883–88.	Castle Malwood, New Forest. Rt. Hon. Sir William Harcourt, Bart.
1886–87.	Mayes, Warnham, nr. Horsham. Arthur Labouchere, Esq.
1883–5.	Sykefield, Leicester. William Harris, Esq.
1886–92.	Woodbastwick Hall, Norfolk. Albemarle Cator, Esq.

The following Houses were enlarged or altered :

Stanmer, Sussex.   Earl of Chichester.

Gopsall Hall, Staffordshire.   Earl Howe.

Mayfield, Surrey.   Lord Penzance.

Pinkney Hall, Norfolk.   J. S. Scott Chad, Esq.

Tortworth Court, Gloucestershire.   Earl of Ducie.

East Hampstead Park, Berks.   Marquis of Downshire, large Conservatory added.

Glyndebourne, Sussex.   W. L. Christie, Esq.

Burcote House, Oxfordshire.   Dowager Countess of Crawford, in progress at the time of his death.

OBITUARY NOTICES.

THE following letter from Mr Macvicar Anderson, a Fellow and former President of the Institute, is printed in the *Journal of the R.I.B.A.* for Feb. 28, 1895.

" But one feeling—a feeling of unaffected sorrow— pervaded the profession on learning of the death of Ewan Christian—a name which for very many years has been universally regarded as the synonym of all that is high-minded and straightforward, not only by architects, but by the outside world. As architect to the Ecclesiastical Commissioners his place will indeed be difficult to fill. All who came in contact with him in this relationship can testify to the rare ability and conscientious devotion with which he unremittingly discharged his duties. Not a few architects will sadly miss the kindly courtesy with which he was wont to offer suggestions, that never failed to be of practical value and to educe grateful acknowledgement. In the exercise of private practice, the confidence and esteem he inspired were such as can only be created by the man of integrity and the

architect of ability. With him age was accompanied
not so much by weakness, as by undaunted energy.
In harness almost to the last, with but a few days of
illness, who could have wished for a more merciful
or a more appropriate close to a prolonged life of
exceptionally earnest work? Simple-minded, true,
and kind of heart, self-reliant, generous, full of enthusiasm such as is rarely to be found unaccompanied by
youth, of wide experience and extensive knowledge,
the veteran of whom we were proud, and whom we
all regarded with real affection, has passed to his
rest, leaving to the profession and to many besides
the heritage of a noble example, none the less valued
because tinged, as for the time it must be, by the
deep feelings of regret and sorrow which all experience who survive him."

The Architectural Journals all contained obituary
notices ; so much of these as consisted of records of
his principal works, similar to that given above by
Mr Birch, have been omitted, but the following comments of professional critics upon his character and
work have a value of their own, and will be read with
interest.

"Mr Ewan Christian has departed from us after
a life which was almost enviable. He had passed his
eightieth year ; he had acquired the respect of the
numerous architects who met him as the representative of the Ecclesiastical Commissioners. It

might be said that the greater part of his life was spent in the exercise of judicial functions, and he fulfilled his duty with a sense of justice which was never surpassed in any of the courts of law. As he once said of himself, " Mine has been a life of independent service, not of exploits. I have undoubtedly done much work, and some, I hope, of a valuable kind to those most interested ; but I could not think of comparing myself with the great architects and archæologists of our own and other countries. My highest ambition has been that of doing to the best of my ability the duty from time to time set before me to accomplish, and of maintaining unsullied in every sense the high character of an honourable and independent architect." These manly and yet modest words expressed an ideal of character which nobody could dare to say was not in keeping with Mr Christian's daily life. He held an onerous office, and he never endeavoured to turn its functions into indirect advantage for himself, as has happened in other times and places. Sometimes he found his duties trying, as when novices, immature or unskilful architects, endeavoured to uphold their notions against his experience, but in the end he generally enjoyed the satisfaction of a rational victory. Mr Christian, in fact, made the duties of his office more onerous to himself, by the pains he bestowed in trying to raise the character of many of the designs submitted to him, and, if it were not for his endeavours, we are afraid a great many churches would have a more unpleasing appearance. His own work, whatever the style, was always in excellent taste, but he could not escape the fate of all critics in the arts. He became over fastidious, and designed as if his powers were restrained. It was as a judge that his keenness, honesty and skill were most apparent. Mr Christian's report on the designs for the Edinburgh Cathedral is a model of its kind. Every line reveals the knowledge of a master who was competent to recommend alterations in the work of the ablest among his contemporaries, and who was not afraid to express his own preference. Many architects have had reason to be grateful to Mr Christian, and we trust the respect for his memory will be expressed in a permanent form."—*The Architect*, March 1, 1895.

"In our obituary column we have given a few particulars as to the life and work of the late Mr Ewan Christian, whose death will be regretted by all who knew him, and who leaves behind him the reputation of an accomplished and conscientious architect and a kind-hearted and courteous gentleman. Mr Christian was nearly 81 at the time of his death, and therefore cannot in one sense be said to have died prematurely, but one cannot but regret that he should not have lived to see the completion and opening of his most important building, the National Portrait Gallery. In the design of this Mr Christian had contrived, with a great deal of judgment, to give a special treatment to the main block of building at the back of the National Gallery, while effecting the juncture of the old and new building on the east side in such a manner as to avoid any clashing with the architectural design of the National Gallery itself. The only point we think rather questionable is the appearance of the assemblage of pediments of different sizes on the intermediate portion of the building, as seen from the east. But the main block is a dignified structure suitable to its position, and if the interior planning and lighting have been carried out, as will probably be found to be the case, in a practically satisfactory manner, the building will be a worthy monument of its architect."—*The Builder*, March 2, 1895.

" At the ripe age of eighty years, full of honours, and with the best secular work he has ever attempted almost completed, Ewan Christian has gone the way of all flesh, and his host of friends in the Architectural world will know him no more. Mr Christian's chief works were his church restorations, and he has restored more churches—under the Ecclesiastical and the Charity Commissioners, for whom he worked religiously for very many years—than any other six men in England. His principal restoration, if one would pick a solitary instance out of many hundreds, was unquestionably the restoration of Southwell Minster, and the rebuilding of its tower ; but his staircase at the National Gallery, and the important additions to the building which have been for several years gradually growing to completion, and which will undoubtedly form a magnificent home for the National Portraits which have been buffetted about the world, to our great dishonour, will call him most to the memory of architectural London. We only hear of his death as we are going to press—time enough, however, to express our sorrow at the loss of such an eminent Church Architect, and such a polished gentleman." *The Builders' Journal*, Feb. 26, 1895.

" We regret to have to record the decease of Mr Ewan Christian, for many years architect to the Ecclesiastical Commissioners. In the year 1887 he was elected as the recipient of the Royal Gold Medal, the president for the year, the late Mr Edward I'Anson, remarking that Mr Christian's 'long and busy life had been spent in conscientious, honourable work, evincing throughout a thorough knowledge of his art, while no architect could have more zealously and faithfully studied the interests of the Ecclesiastical Commissioners.' In replying, Mr Christian said : 'Mine has been a life of independent service, not of exploits. My highest ambition has been that of doing to the best of my ability the duty from time to time set before me to accomplish, and of maintaining unsullied in every sense the high character of an honourable and independent architect.' These two sentences give a fair epitome of the character of the architect who has just passed away. In no sense a heaven-born genius, or even possessed of brilliant parts, but a man of inflexible honesty, great industry, and good business capabilities, he was a safe man, who would fulfil to the best of his powers any work committed to him. Many are the stories current of the pains he would take to explain to young architects the defects in their designs, and the way in which they might be amended, when plans for new rectories or mission churches were submitted for his official approval, and many have profited by the apparently harsh, but well-grounded criticism, rapidly delivered in nervous, almost irritable, tones. A sequel to his three years' occupancy of the carved 'lions' chair at 9, Conduit-street, was that a subscription portrait of Mr Christian was painted by Mr W. W. Ouless, R.A., and was presented to the Institute in February, 1888." —*The Building News*, March 1, 1895.

Thwaitehead Hampstead Heath.

CHAPTER III.

CHARACTER.

"𝕾𝖆𝖑𝖚𝖘 𝖕𝖊𝖗 𝕮𝖍𝖗𝖎𝖘𝖙𝖚𝖒."

"𝕿𝖗𝖚𝖘𝖙 𝖆𝖓𝖉 𝕾𝖙𝖗𝖎𝖛𝖊."

THE name of *Christian*, scattered up and down in the records of the old Kingdom of Man during many centuries, and still commonly borne by many people of the Island, takes us back to a distant age when a man who professed the faith of Christ was marked and noted, for good or ill, among his heathen neighbours, and bore the reproach of Christ in his very name[1]. At a later date, when men began to distinguish families by heraldic devices, the family of Christian, rejoicing in the possession of a name, the reproach of which had long ceased, took for their appropriate cognizance *three sacramental cups*, with the motto, *Salus per Christum*.

[1] The name is thought to have reached the Island from the Danish Colonies in Ireland, but this is uncertain. Another Manx name of similar meaning is *Mylchreest*, from MacGuilley Chreest—'the son of Christ's servant.'

Of the latest member of this family whom God has called to his rest in a ripe old age, it may be permitted to others to say that he was not unworthy the full significance of his honourable name, and that the ancient family motto was the guiding principle of his life. *Salus per Christum*—whatever the natural grace and strength of his character, however manfully he strove to do his duty towards God and his neighbour, he counted all for nought, and for acceptance with God looked to the merits of Christ alone. The opening clause of his will—a document in which a man may be supposed to disclose his character to posterity—expresses his simple faith in words of such unaffected pathos and so entirely his own, that we transcribe them in full.

"Sinful and unholy as I know myself to be, and only fit to loathe myself and repent in dust and ashes, yet I trust I may die in the unclouded faith that in His one all-sufficient sacrifice Jesus Christ made an atonement for me, and that unworthy, utterly unworthy, as I am, His precious blood-shedding will cleanse and purify and make me meet to wear the white robe of His righteousness in the great assembly of His saints. Amen! Amen!"

Such, in few words, was his creed, but it was one which touched his conduct at all points, and made his whole life to glow with the force of vital religion. Deeply penetrated with the conviction that all which he had, of natural gift or acquired by his own industry, all his 'safety' from peril to soul or body, was the gift of God 'through Christ,' he reckoned nothing that he had his own, but did all his service 'as to the Lord and not to men,' setting the Lord always before him, whether at home or abroad, in hours of business or in moments of relaxation. Thus it can hardly be said of him that there was what is sometimes called 'a religious side' to his character, for his religion was on all sides, behind not a whit less than before. He had opinions of his own, clearly defined and well matured, upon Church questions, being an old-fashioned Evangelical, or as one of the few surviving friends of his early years[1] has said, "he adhered to his old-fashioned Puritan predilections to the last," but the same friend adds, that "he was singularly free from anything like bigotry," adducing in proof his liberal support of a certain hospital for children, founded under auspices very remote from Puritan. He was indeed wholly free from the spirit of party strife, but he loved the Church of England and her Prayer Book and her Catechism with all his heart, and he was an Evangelical because he believed that the doctrine and the simplicity of worship presented under that name were the truest interpretation of the mind of the Church. So he would always speak of "the Communion Table," just because that was the name which he considered to be authorized by the

---

[1] Mr Thomas C. Hine, of Nottingham, Architect.

Prayer Book, and much as he loved beauty in church architecture, he contented himself for five-and-forty years with his seat in St John's Chapel, Downshire Hill, one of the old Proprietary Chapels in which the eye bears little part in lifting the heart to devotion. There, Sunday by Sunday, until the last week of his life, was seen his earnest countenance, with its lines of thought, its prominent brow and crown of silvery hair. True to the oft-repeated maxims of his favourite author, George Herbert (whose church at Leighton Bromswold he restored [1] with loving care), he was a time-mark for his friends as he walked to church up Haverstock Hill, often telling his family, "Stay not for t'other pin"; and there even in old age he reverently kneeled, again quoting the same authority for devout worship, "Kneeling ne'er spoiled silk stockings." In the Sunday-school of St John's too he was Teacher and Superintendent for thirty-five years, no stress of weather, no toils or cares of the busy week, ever interrupting the performance of his office. In this, as in everything else, his work was marked by that regularity and method [2] which he could honestly require from others because he set such a noble example. At home he always read the *Christian*

---

[1] He took especial pleasure in placing the pulpit and desk at even height, as the poet-priest had designed, so that neither preaching nor praying should be exalted above the other.

[2] See the note by the Rev. J. Kirkman on p. 47.

Year for the day, and sometimes Herbert's *Poems*, which, with the *Pilgrim's Progress*, Walton's *Lives*, Matthew Henry's *Commentary* (a portion of which he studied daily in his later years), and more recently some of Bishop Westcott's and Bishop Phillips Brooks' writings, formed his favourite reading.

Thus peacefully passed the sacred rest-days of his busy life, his reverence for Sunday being a principle which he steadily maintained, at home or abroad, in whatever company he might be. But this did not constitute his religion, being only one expression of it, and known to few but his own friends at Hampstead, for he would always strive so to arrange his work in the week that he might have his Sunday at home. But strengthened in heart by these fresh springs of service of the sanctuary, or of secret communion with God, he went forth to do each day's work in such manner that none could doubt Whose he was or Whom he served. As one who knew him intimately in professional relations[1] once remarked, 'Mr Christian carried his religion into everything he did.'

It is not known when or from what source Mr Christian adopted that other motto, which stands at the head of this chapter—" Trust and strive,"—but the words were frequently on his lips ; from the windows of his office they met the eye of all who came to see him there, and they are prominent among the words of wisdom which adorn the walls of his own house.

---

[1] Mr Burford, of Hampstead, Builder.

'Trust' he did indeed—humbly, heartily, wholly; he never left his house in the morning, never entered a railway carriage (for a long journey) without baring his head reverently, though almost secretly, for a brief commendatory prayer. But this secret 'trust' in God's providence was parallel to, and closely connected with, 'striving,'—with that splendid profusion of energy, which made him, as a brother architect[1] said, "an example to the young men of untiring energy, as well as of professional dignity." An architect by the choice of his boyhood, he was indeed the architect of his own fortunes. Orphaned of both parents before he was eight years old, he entered an architect's office at the age of 15, and without money or influence made his onward way by honest and faithful work, until he attained the honourable position of President and Gold Medallist of the Royal Institute of British Architects. To the story of his early hardships and struggles he used sometimes to refer in after years, with honest satisfaction that he had been enabled to make his own way in life, and proportionately indignant with any who sought to shorten their road to success by reliance upon the influence of others rather than their own exertions. Any such use of favour was utterly distasteful to him, and great as were the opportunities of influence which his official position afforded, he never made use of them either to advance his own interests or

[1] Mr W. Swinden Barber, of Sheffield.

to benefit[1] relatives or friends. Writing (in 1855) to his eldest brother John, with whom he had lived during the years that he was learning his profession, he says that he has been reckoning up how much his maintenance had cost, and wishes to repay him the whole amount, adding that this confers on him the proud satisfaction of feeling that from the age of nine he has cost his family nothing, and that he has not a sixpence in the world that is not the result of God's blessing on his own honest industry.

This was no idle boast; his industry was habitual, continuous, incessant; from the autumn day in 1829 when he entered Mr Habershon's office as a pupil, he may be said to have worked at his profession without intermission, until that cold day in the long frost of February, 1895, when he left his office in Whitehall Place, within five brief days to enter the "city which hath foundations, whose builder and maker is God."

He was fond of relating how he rose early on his wedding morning to make a report on a church, and when full 80 years old he climbed into the roof of a church with such steady eye and active foot as surprised the younger men who held the ladder below. Even in his summer holidays the same ceaseless activity pervaded all his movements, sometimes to an extent which caused amusement to his friends. "Where is Mr Christian?" said one of a party on a Highland tour, during the passage of the boat

---

[1] See Mr Birch's remarks upon his rigid impartiality, on p. 60.

through a lock on the Caledonian Canal, which permitted the passengers to land for a few minutes, and gaze from the hill-side on the fair mountain prospect. "Oh, I don't know," was the reply of Mr Chalk[1], a frequent companion of his travels, though preferring to take his amusements with more of repose than suited Mr Christian's temperament, "he was here just now, said it was glorious, and was off again."

But it should not be supposed that this ceaseless activity, continuing into years when most men seek repose in honourable retirement from service, was occasioned by a desire to add to the comforts of life or to accumulate a fortune. He had indeed excellent opportunities for doing so, had this been his object, through his official position, but in truth he loved to do honest work, which should bring glory to God and be serviceable to the Church and to his fellow-men. To a friend[2], telling him of a man who inherited a good fortune, but, having a large family, stinted himself and them with the idea of leaving to each as much as he had received, he replied with the vigorous declaration, "What a fool!" and then proceeded to enforce his conviction that work, and the performance of duty, and the enjoyment of God's free gifts were the essential conditions of a happy life, with which money had little to do.

[1] Secretary to the Ecclesiastical Commission, afterwards Sir James G. Chalk.

[2] Mr Basil Woodd Smith, of Hampstead, J. P.

It certainly had little to do with his happiness; whether his work brought him gain or loss—and the latter was no uncommon occurrence through his unwillingness to press clients for payment, where church funds were low—whether it added to his credit with men or not, was to him a very small matter, so as good work was accomplished, work that would last, and be of service to generations yet to come. "That," said a builder to him once, "will stand for a life-time." "That won't do for me," was Mr Christian's reply, "I want all my work to stand for 300 years."

Such was his energy, known of all who had to do with him; and his energy was accompanied or controlled, as was equally well known, by the highest integrity of purpose, by unswerving devotion to the strict path of duty, by perfect candour in thought and word. On no point in his character is there such a consent of witness from many friends who have written words of condolence. "Certainly," writes one clergyman[1], after acknowledging that he had differed with him more than once in professional matters—"certainly whatever he did, he did because he thought it right, and no lower motive had place in his calculations." "I owe to him," writes one[2] who had been in his office, "my early impressions in life of what constituted the duty of an architect. He was the very soul of honour, and I always looked up to him

[1] Author of an obituary notice in the *Church Times* for 15 March, 1895.
[2] Mr F. Chancellor, of Chelmsford, Architect.

as the 'Bayard' of our profession." His rugged independence and fearless honesty, inherited perhaps from his Cumbrian ancestors, were manifest in all that he did, and found a reflection, so to speak, in the style and form of his architecture. He was ever for solid work, the same all round, and he hated buildings with pretentious front of stone, but sides of brick. A gentleman who had engaged him to build a house used to say in after years that he had almost despaired of ever seeing it rise above the ground, since Mr Christian made the builders take up the foundations three times before he was satisfied that they were duly laid. He was indeed a relentless foe to any who tried to shirk their duty or scamp their work, and punished such practices unsparingly, as when climbing to the top of a church tower, and finding that inferior materials were being used, contrary to his express directions, he pulled the turret to pieces with his own hands, and flung the rubble down into the churchyard, much to the dismay of the builders. The perfect transparency of his character found expression also in his well-known love of sunshine, which he was always planning to bring into church or house. "Ove non viene il sole, viene il medico," was a favourite maxim with him, and he used to delight to tell into how many vicarages throughout the country he had contrived to introduce the bright sunshine. He acted as judge in the competition for building the new Training College at Norwich, for which a large number of designs were sent in, and one of the Committee[1] relates how being asked at the public opening of the College what it was that led him to give the preference to the plan which he had selected, he answered at once, " My love of abundant light." Truly indeed has it been said that " his soul loved honesty and candour, as he loved light and air and breadth of sky and openness to the eye of the sun." Or in the words of another intimate friend[2], " he was intolerant of cobwebs and stagnation, and had no dark corners in which the light was not welcome." He loved to come to the light, because he loved to do the truth.

In manner Mr Christian was naturally somewhat reserved, and his natural shyness had perhaps been increased by the loneliness of many years of his earlier life, the effect of which he never quite shook off. He had a wonderful control of speech, never opening his mouth, unless he had something to say which he thought should be said. But his 'conversation' or conduct was eloquent, even when his lips were closed. One of those[2] who enjoyed his companionship and guidance[3] in foreign travel, and who set high value on

---

[1] Canon Hinds Howell, Rector of Drayton, Norwich.

[2] Mr Basil Woodd Smith.

[3] He seemed naturally to lead the way in all expeditions, a habit to which a lady makes very happy allusion in a letter written on hearing of his death; " in the old days he was always a little way in front. I think it is the same now as it has always been—he is a little way in front."

both, relates how one morning at Mürren he came upon him reading his Bible on the mountain-side, and how this simple incident deeply impressed him, revealing the man more clearly than volumes of religious talk would have done. He was undoubtedly a man of action rather than of speech, and when he spoke he had a natural tendency to take the side of opposition, in a way which often caused amusement to his friends. In the course of the Highland tour of 1870, to which allusion has been made before, the question arose whether the party should take the coach or the steamer route from Oban. Mr Chalk wished for the steamer, as the less fatiguing mode of travelling, but Mr Christian, who always laid out the route for his companions, decided for the coach. "Ah," said Mr Chalk to the third member of the party, " I ought to have gone in for the coach, and then we should have got the steamer." But in matters of serious import, he never opposed without good reason. It cannot indeed be denied, that he had, as one of his oldest friends[1] has said, " a profound belief in his own opinion," and a very decided preference for his own judgment, which to those who did not understand him might sometimes bear the appearance of mere contrariety; but this is easily understood when it is remembered that from early years he had been accustomed to form his own judgment and shape his own course, and so he never spoke without having

[1] Mr Thomas C. Hine.

previously thought out the subject; "he knew his own mind, and was not to be coaxed or scolded out of it," said one[1] who knew him well. And naturally this carefully formed opinion took shape in steadfast purpose and deliberate action, such as may be read in the character of his signature—every letter clear and bold at the age of 80, as in his diaries written more than 50 years before.

" The greater part of his life had been spent," says the writer of an obituary notice in the *Architect*, " in the exercise of judicial functions, and he fulfilled his duty with a sense of justice which was never surpassed in any of the Courts of Law ;" and the justice which he meted to others he rigorously applied to his own conduct. It was his rule to make good out of his own pocket, and sometimes at very heavy cost, any defects in building, the blame for which rested in any degree upon himself, or could not be brought home to the defaulter, and often he used to take the blame to himself in cases where others would have been dis- posed to acquit him.

Nor was it only in professional relations that this love of justice was apparent. In all family matters he was scrupulously careful to hold an even balance between his children; the first money which he earned in his profession he devoted to repaying his elder brother what had been spent on his education, and among the many acts of generosity which the compe-

[1] The writer of the notice in the *Church Times.*

tence of later years enabled him to perform, none probably gave him greater pleasure than acknowledging his indebtedness to his old school by purchasing the position of Governor of Christ's Hospital.

It may be, however, that some who read these words will hardly recognize the truth of what we have said of Mr Christian's reserve and silence, having listened to his animated and richly instructive conversation. The truth is that he had an enthusiastic love of all that was good and true and beautiful, with a corresponding detestation of anything false or foul, and the sight or even the mention of either quickly opened his lips, and let loose a flow of unstinted generous admiration, or of unsparing and vehement condemnation. Often when reading his newspaper in the evening, while others were engaged in conversation, if his eye or ear caught mention of any deed of thoughtful kindness or chivalrous self-denial, he would loudly applaud; just as in climbing a Swiss mountain, when past 70 years of age, he would wave his hat wildly and shout " Hurrah," as a turn in the path revealed some fresh loveliness of prospect. " No man's enthusiasm ever kept pace with his years, as Mr Christian's did," is the remark of one of his brother architects[1].

Another feature of his character known well by those who did know him—who, as another architect[2]

---

[1] Mr Waterhouse, R.A. late President R.I.B.A.
[2] Mr F. C. Penrose, President of the R.I.B.A.

said, "were illumined by his kindly presence"—though perhaps to some extent veiled from others by the same reserve of which we have spoken, was the deep kindliness of his heart, and generous readiness to help those who were in distress, or to promote schemes of public usefulness. "I always teach my sons to *save*," said a leading member of his profession to him ; "and I," was the reply, "teach my daughters to *give*." These alms-deeds were often done so secretly that none but the recipients of his bounty knew whence they came, nor indeed did they always know ; near the close of his life one of his friends received a large donation for a certain object in which both were interested, with the significant inscription on the envelope—"Silence."

But his genuine kindness of heart was manifest in various forms to all who had to do with him. It was manifest in the way in which he used to speak of others, for he never would permit himself to repeat any evil on mere hearsay. It was manifest in all his dealings with those in his office or whom he met in business. "A kinder heart," says one of his former assistants[1], "underlying that sort of reserve which so often is characteristic of the noblest natures, I have never met"; another of his pupils[2]—whose prolonged "engagement faded out like the light of a happy summer's day"—bears his record, "next to my own

---

[1] Mr A. H. Haig, Artist.
[2] Mr A. R. Barker, Architect, Diocesan Surveyor for Winchester.

father he always was to me the kindest friend I
possessed"; and a builder[1] with whom he had many
business relations, adds similar testimony—" I can
never have another earthly friend so great as he has
been to me."

We have spoken of Mr Christian's untiring energy,
and continued application to the work of his profession, from the dawn of manhood to the sunset of
his long life; this was evident even to those who
knew him least, but it would be a mistake to suppose
that he cared for nothing else than architecture. To
the amusements and sports in which many hard-
working men seek for recreation, he was indeed wholly
indifferent, but he had other delights to which he
was wont to recur for refreshment of wearied body
and mind. Of his love of his home and family it
may suffice to repeat what has been said above, that
however far a-field his duties called him in the week,
he always endeavoured to return on Sunday to
" Thwaitehead"—his house which he had built on
Hampstead Heath, and which with filial piety he
named after the old Cumbrian home of that mother
whom he lost so early, but whose memory he
cherished and honoured to the last. Though known
as a friend in need by so many, he had not a
large circle of intimate friends, but those admitted
within that circle were tenants for life, and he loved
their fellowship and conversation. Those whom he

---

[1] Mr J. Gaymer, of North Walsham.

used to invite year by year to share in the commemoration of his wedding-day, will not soon forget those delightful excursions by road or river—the characteristic order of all the arrangements, the thoughtful provision for the comfort of every guest, young or old, the genial and abundant hospitality which formed the outward expression of his deep thankfulness for the great joy of his life. On such occasions, as well as in longer summer excursions to his ancestral Lake-land, or among Scotch mountains, or the snows of Switzerland, or even in a brief walk before breakfast on Hampstead Heath, it was seen how his spirit found refreshment in the contemplation of Nature in all her varying moods, and, as a kindly mother, Nature repaid her dutiful child by endowing him with length of years and robust health and wonderful vigour of mind and body.

This endeavour faithfully to pourtray the character of a man of whom one[1] who knew him well in his professional life for many years, has said, "so near an approach to an ideal man in any capacity never came within my cognizance," although a pleasant task, a very labour of love, yet has not been an easy matter, even for one whose high privilege and lasting responsibility it was to share for nearly a quarter of a century in the sacred peace and joy of his family life.

If it were required to find one word in which to

---

[1] Sir George Pringle, late Secretary to the Ecclesiastical Commission.

present such a character, we should claim, without fear of contradiction from any who ever knew him, that he was a *gentleman*. If asked to give some explanation of the sense in which we used that much-abused word, we should reply by quoting the following letter[1] written by him :—

" Mr Bright is reported to have said that members of Parliament should be 'gentleman-like men.' The writer tenders his respectful compliments, but thinks he should have said ' gentlemen '; possibly he has been wrongly reported. 'Gentleman-like' may cover something really very bad at heart, and cannot be depended on when the trial comes; but the *true* gentleman, as described in the lines written on the accompanying page, whether he be peer or peasant, rich or poor, is always sure to be found on the right side."

" The picture of a *true gentleman*, as described by a king who had once been a shepherd."

Lord, who shall abide in Thy tabernacle ? who shall dwell in Thy holy hill ?

He that walketh uprightly, and worketh righteousness, and speaketh the truth in his heart.

He that backbiteth not with his tongue, nor doeth evil to his neighbour, nor taketh up a reproach against his neighbour.

In whose eyes a vile person is contemned; but he honoureth them that fear the LORD. He that sweareth to his own hurt, and changeth not.

---

[1] The letter seems never to have been sent.

He that putteth not out his money to usury, nor taketh reward against the innocent. He that doeth these things shall never be moved.

This Psalm he constantly set before others as a rule of life ; those who now mourn his loss and venerate his memory, can testify how faithful his endeavours to follow the same rule himself; how near his approach to it may be said only by Him who searcheth the heart, and " who will reward to every man according to his deeds : to them who by patient continuance in well-doing seek for glory and honour and immortality, eternal life." Amen.

MURAL LEGENDS.

It was an old fancy of Mr Christian's—"a very wholesome custom," as he called it—to adorn the walls of buildings with texts of Holy Scripture or other words of the wise ; and those painted or moulded on the windows and walls of his own house and office were so carefully selected with regard to the purpose of the rooms, and even the aspect of the walls, that his own character seems to speak in the words of his choice.

Thwaitehead

OVER THE FRONT DOOR

Benedic anima mea Domino. Amen.
1848.　E. A. C.　1882.

(The dates of his marriage and of building the house—the foundation of the family and of their abode.)

On the Porch

Pax intrantibus—salus exeuntibus.

ROUND THE OUTER WALLS

(*Near the entrance*) God's Providence is mine inheritance. Through wisdom is an house builded, but except the Lord build the house their labour is but lost that build it. (*West side*) At evening time it shall be light. (*South side*) The heavens declare the glory of God, and truly the light is sweet, and a pleasant thing it is for the eyes to behold the sun. All Thy works praise Thee, O Lord, and to those (*East side*) that fear Thy Name shall the Sun of righteousness arise. Ewan Christian, Architect, Robinson Cornish, John Gaymer, W. Richardson, built this house. (*North side*) Peace be to all those who now or hereafter herein shall dwell. Amen.

IN THE HALL

ON THE DOOR

Welcome the coming, speed the parting guest.

ON THE WINDOW

Trust and strive.	Salus per Christum.	Trust and strive.
Honour all men.	Love as brethren.	Speak no guile.
Be pitiful.	Be, not seem to be.	Be courteous.

ON THE CHIMNEY-PIECE

Fear God, honour the King.

ROUND THE CORNICE

He prayeth well, who loveth well both man and bird and beast. He prayeth best, who loveth best all things both great and small; for the dear God who loveth us, He made and loveth all.

IN THE DRAWING ROOM

On the North Window

Life is real, Life is earnest.
Still achieving, still pursuing,
Learn to labour and to wait.

On the South Window

Let your speech be always with grace.
A word fitly spoken, how good is it.

On the West Window,

Overlooking the seat in Well-walk on which the poet Keats used to sit, these words taken from two of his Sonnets, and from 'Endymion.'

The poetry of earth is never dead.
Unnumbered sounds that evening store,
The songs of birds, the whispering of the leaves,
Make pleasing music.

A thing of beauty is a joy for ever;
Its loveliness increases; it will never
Pass into nothingness, but still will keep
A bower quiet for us.

IN THE DINING ROOM

On the East Window

Prayer and provender hindereth no man.
Eat thy bread with joy, giving thanks.
A contented mind is a continual feast.

On the South Window

Be thrifty, but not covetous.
Give thy honour and thy friend his due.

Round the Cornice

Be useful where thou livest. Find out men's wants and will and meet them there. All worldly joys go less to the one joy of doing kindnesses. Thy friend put in thy bosom; wear his eyes still in thy heart, that he may see what's there.

IN THE LIBRARY

On the Window

Studies serve for delight.
Let knowledge grow from more to more.
Knowledge is power.

On the Chimney-Piece

Silence is golden.

ROUND THE CORNICE

Love all: trust a few: do wrong to none:
keep thy friend under thy own life's key.
This above all: to thine own self be true,
and it must follow, as the night the day,
thou canst not then be false to any man.

At his Office in Whitehall Place.

IN HIS OWN ROOM.

ON THE CORNICE, FACING MR CHRISTIAN AS HE SAT AT HIS TABLE

Trust in the Lord with all thine heart, and lean not to thine own understanding. In all thy ways acknowledge Him, and He shall direct thy paths. Be not wise in thine own eyes.

FACING THE CLIENT WHO CAME TO CONSULT HIM

Through wisdom is an house builded, and by understanding it is established, and by knowledge shall the chambers be filled with all pleasant and precious riches.

ON THE CROSS-BEAM

Let him that thinketh he standeth take heed lest he fall.

ON THE CHIMNEY-PIECE

Whatsoever thy hand findeth to do, do with thy might. Not with eye service.

On the Cornice

In all labour there is profit, but through idleness of the hands the house droppeth through. Prepare thy work without and make it fit for thyself in the field, and afterwards build thine house. The blessing of the Lord it maketh rich, and He addeth no sorrow with it.

Under the Skylight

(*East, south and west sides*) Truly the light is sweet and a pleasant thing it is for the eyes to behold the sun. (*North side*) Ove non viene il sole, viene il medico.